BEYOND THE SUNSET

When Penelope Jones was offered a job as nanny on the tiny island of Torvaig, off the West Coast of Scotland, she was anxious to take it for more than one reason. The most urgent was to 'get away from it all'—and from the heartbreak of a love affair that had gone wrong. And she was fascinated by the fact that her forebears had come from Torvaig and this would be her first chance to see the place for herself. But she soon discovered that her new employer, the formidable laird of Torvaig, didn't believe any of her reasons!

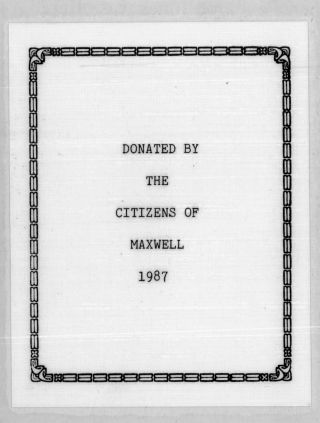

DONATED BY

THE

CITIZENS OF

MAXWELL

1987

075101

BEYOND THE SUNSET

Flora Kidd

ATLANTIC LARGE PRINT
Chivers Press, Bath, England.
John Curley & Associates Inc.,
South Yarmouth, Mass., USA.

Library of Congress Cataloging in Publication Data

Kidd, Flora.
 Beyond the sunset.

 (Atlantic large print)
 Reprint. Originally published: London: Mills & Boon, 1973.
 1. Large type books.   I. Title.
 [PR9199.3.K4287B4 1985]   813'.54   84–19953
 ISBN 0–89340–832–8 (J. Curley: lg. print)

British Library Cataloguing in Publication Data

Kidd, Flora
 Beyond the sunset.—Large print ed.—
 (Atlantic large print books)
 I. Title
 823'.914[F]   PR6061.I/

 ISBN 0–7451–9019–7   *8752829*

This Large Print edition is published by Chivers Press, England, and
John Curley & Associates, Inc, U.S.A. 1985

Published by arrangement with Mills & Boon Limited

U.K. Hardback ISBN 0 7451 9019 7
U.S.A. Softback ISBN 0 89340 832 8

© Flora Kidd 1973

9.95

. . . My purpose holds
To sail beyond the sunset, and the baths
Of all the western stars, until I die.
It may be that the gulfs will wash us down;
It may be we shall touch the Happy Isles.

TENNYSON: *Ulysses*

BEYOND THE SUNSET

All the characters in this book have no existence outside the imagination of the Author, and have no relation whatsoever to anyone bearing the same name or names. They are not even distantly inspired by any individual known or unknown to the Author, and all the incidents are pure invention.

CHAPTER ONE

The day Penelope Jones arrived at Mallaig, a fishing port on the north-west coast of Scotland, was bright with the sunshine of mid-August. Not a breath of air stirred as she stood on the quayside and looked about her in delighted fascination at a scene which was strange to her eyes.

The fishing fleet was in and the sturdy boats, some varnished, some painted green or black, with high bows and spiky radio masts, jostled each other beside the stone wall of the quay. Derricks swung and creaked as the catch was lifted out of deep holds. Seagulls and terns swooped and screeched, tormented by the sight and smell of so many silvery, netted fish.

Beyond the boats the water of the harbour was a deep blue, reflecting the serene cloudless sky which arched above greyish-green curves of treeless hills. Several sailing yachts, a-swing at their anchor chains, nodded in narcissistic admiration of their reflections on the smooth water. The air was tangy with the smell of herrings being kippered in nearby

1

sheds, where wood chippings, used in the fires, were piled on the floor like heaps of golden cereal.

Turning away from the kippering sheds Penelope caught her breath as she saw for the first time, across an expanse of glittering sea, the dark serrated peaks of the mountains of Skye, those magical, mysterious heaps of rock, which had dominated the stories told by her grandmother, who had been born on an island called Torvaig, one of the Inner Hebrides, lying further to the north of Skye.

Excitement flared suddenly through Penelope. The feeling was unusual because she was normally a calm girl, who prided herself on being able to keep her cool in most situations as befitted a children's nanny. But this was the first time she had been to the Highlands of Scotland, and, since she considered them to be her spiritual home, a little excitement was to be expected.

She swung round again to look at the harbour and her eyes were caught by the glitter of chromium-plated fittings on a big two-masted yacht which was anchored near the entrance to the harbour. It seemed to her to be as flagrant an example of affluence as anything she had seen during her journey north that morning and she wondered who owned it.

But instead of standing and staring she should be looking for the person who had come to meet her. Slim and neat in her navy blue trouser suit, she turned again and walked briskly to the white building where the harbourmaster had his office.

She was just about to turn the handle of the door when it opened and a young man walked out, almost knocking her down. Big hands grasped her shoulders, to prevent her from falling, and a pair of roguish brown eyes laughed down at her.

'Well now, I wasn't expecting to walk into someone like you. I hope I didn't hurt you?'

His voice was deep and had a lilt to it. His hair was red-gold and was long enough to lap the neckband of his sweater. He was also wearing sailcloth trousers tucked into short rubber boots. He was big and handsome and she judged his age to be the same as her own. She decided he must be a fisherman off one of the boats.

'I'm all right, thank you,' she replied, rather primly, very conscious that his

3

hands were still on her shoulders, and that the roguish glint in his eyes had increased, as his glance wandered over her flushed cheeks, shining dark hair and trim figure.

'I've just arrived here and I'm expecting to be met at this office,' she explained.

His eyes widened incredulously and his hands slid from her shoulders. He folded his arms across his wide chest and stared down at her.

'You can't be Miss Jones from London?' he said in awed tones.

'Yes, my name is Penelope Jones,' she answered. 'I'm on my way to Torvaig.'

'And I'm the one sent to meet you at the harbourmaster's office,' he murmured, obviously still incredulous. He held out one of his big hands. 'Hugh Drummond, at your service, Miss Jones. You can't possibly be a nanny. Nannies are middle-aged and unshaped. They wear the most awfully frumpy clothes and funny hats with round brims, and they nearly always carry umbrellas.'

'Not these days,' replied Penelope, with a grin which made her eyes sparkle and produced two dimples in her soft cheeks. 'I'm pleased to meet you, Mr. Drummond. My luggage is over there. Where is your

4

car?'

He gave her piled luggage a cursory glance and then looked at her. Mischief began to dance in his eyes again.

'I haven't a car here,' he said.

'Then how will we get to Torvaig?' she demanded. Being very efficient herself she sometimes grew a little impatient with what she considered to be inefficiency in others.

'By sailing yacht. Have you ever been in one before?' he asked.

'Never.'

'Then it's just as well the weather is calm for you.' He put back his head and let out a crack of laughter. 'I can hardly wait to see Tearlach's face when he sees you.'

'Tearlach?' she repeated questioningly. The name sounded strange, almost foreign, to her ears.

'It's the Gaelic name meaning Charles, but he's Tearlach to his people, some of whom still speak Gaelic.'

'His people!' exclaimed Penelope. 'Who is he? You make him sound like a feudal lord.'

'Which is the last thing he would claim to be,' murmured Hugh. 'He's the head of our section of the Gunn clan, and on Torvaig his word is law because he owns

5

the island.'

'Then who is Mrs. Drummond, who wrote to me?' asked Penelope, who was thoroughly mystified by her new acquaintance's statements. 'I thought she must be the owner of the island.'

'She would like to be, and thought she would be for a time. But Tearlach turned up, the long-lost son of Murdoch Gunn, laird of Torvaig. Murdoch inherited the island from his great-uncle, but never had the guts or the money to do anything for the island. Anyway, after eighteen years of wandering about the world Tearlach turned up to claim his paltry inheritance.'

'I wouldn't call an island paltry,' objected Penelope.

'You would if you'd seen it when Tearlach took it over. Houses were in ruins, the land was unfarmed and the big house was falling down. It's very different now.'

Penelope had heard of islands being bought by wealthy industrialists and being restored to life. Already she was building in her mind the image of a rotund, kindly-eyed, middle-aged philanthropist who had used his wealth to improve the island of her dreams.

'He came back, like Ulysses, the Last of the Heroes, to claim what was rightly his,' she murmured dreamily, and Hugh gave her a surprised glance.

'I didn't know nannies went in for classical education,' he remarked.

'I don't know Greek or Latin, but I've read the tales of the Greek heroes in translations.'

'And being called Penelope you'd naturally be interested in Ulysses,' teased Hugh. 'All the more reason why I should warn you about my cousin Tearlach.'

'Cousin?' repeated Penelope, thinking she was falling into a habit of repeating everything he said. But she was puzzled by his oblique references to the owner of Torvaig, of whom she had never heard before, and she had to use some means to make him stop and explain.

'Sort of cousin,' he amended. 'Cousin umpteen times removed. My mother's father and Tearlach's father were second cousins and so that makes me and Tearlach. . . .'

'All right,' interrupted Penelope, laughingly. 'I understand. In some way you and he are related. And your mother is the Mrs. Drummond who wrote to me.'

'Yes. Now, as I was saying, don't make the mistake of thinking Tearlach is a classical hero. He's very much of the twentieth century, and he's been a bit of a ruffian in his time. His father was no good and did nothing to uphold the good name of Gunn. Tearlach grew up in one of the poorer areas of Glasgow and learned to hold his own against all comers at an early age. Although he's acquired a veneer of civilisation, there are times when the veneer cracks and the roughness shows both in his speech and his behaviour.'

'Well, whose children am I coming to look after? His?' asked Penelope.

'Ach, no. They're his sister's. After the car crash my mother found a nanny for them, a Miss Swan from Inverness. But she's blotted her copybook in several ways, as far as Tearlach is concerned. She's not been able to control wee Davy and she's talked too much around the island about Tearlach's affairs. Anyway, when Mother was visiting Torvaig recently, Swannie said she'd had enough and gave notice. Tearlach said he'd have to find another nanny, one who wouldn't twitter at him like Swannie does, when he roars at her, and Mother took it upon herself to find someone

8

sensible and responsible. But I'm afraid when he sees you Tearlach is going to be more than surprised. You're not what he had in mind at all.'

'I'm sensible and responsible, I don't gossip and I don't get the twitters when some arrogant man roars at me,' replied Penelope coolly. 'Neither you nor your cousin seem to have the slightest knowledge about trained nannies. Do you think they're all born middle-aged? I can assure you I'm properly trained and I have a diploma. I've already held a similar position to a Very Important Person in London. I have excellent references which your mother must have seen before she recommended me to Mr. Gunn—your cousin.'

Hugh held his arms above his head in a mocking gesture of surrender.

'I give in,' he said with a laugh. 'Please don't misunderstand me. I'm glad you're young and pretty. I live on Torvaig, too, and it's nice to know that someone like yourself is coming there. Still, Tearlach won't be pleased when he sees how young you are and his reception might be extremely hostile and cool.'

'Don't worry about me, Mr.

Drummond. I won't let him put me off. I'm used to dealing with cool customers,' replied Penelope confidently, straightening her slim shoulders and tilting her rounded chin. The sunlight picked out glints of blue and gold in her smooth, shoulder-length dark hair and a gleam of admiration twinkled in Hugh's eyes as he surveyed her.

'I'm thinking you're a cool customer yourself,' he said. 'We won't waste any more time. I'll just tell the harbourmaster I've found you and then we'll load the luggage into the dinghy and be away to the yacht.'

The dinghy was a sturdy clinker boat, painted white, and it had an outboard engine. Quelling her fear of the water and hiding it under her habitual mask of composure, Penelope climbed slowly down the iron ladder set into the stone wall of the quay and stepped into the slightly rocking boat. She sat in the bow, as instructed by Hugh, and soon she was having a different entrancing view of the harbour and town.

Hugh handled the dinghy with the careless ease of one used to messing about in boats most of his life, and steered it towards the big two-masted yacht Penelope had noticed earlier. He took the dinghy alongside the yacht and stopped it beside a small ladder.

Looking up at the gleaming white hull of the yacht, Penelope once more felt the surge of excitement she had felt on shore. Hugh stopped the engine and when all was quiet he yelled, 'Tearlach? We're here!'

Penelope's spurt of excitement changed to a feeling of apprehension. She had not realised she was about to meet the 'cool customer' quite so soon. Collecting all her hard-won poise about her, she followed Hugh's instructions on how she should get out of the dinghy and on to the ladder, and then climbed carefully on to the deck. There she waited and watched Hugh heave her luggage aboard before he came aboard himself to tie the dinghy to the stern of the yacht.

Uncertain as to what she should do next, she stood on the side-deck holding with one hand to a stiff wire, which seemed to be part of the rigging of the main mast. The deck was made of strips of teak laid closely together and it was scrubbed clean so that it was almost white. The other woodwork, she could see, was also teak, but was golden in colour, in marked contrast to the white

11

paintwork of the yacht. The chromium-plated fittings, which she had noticed glittering in the sunlight, were dazzlingly bright at close quarters.

'Sit down,' invited Hugh, pointing to the cushioned bench seats around the cockpit, and feeling a little strange, she did as he suggested. Yachts and all their equipment were a completely new world to her and she sat, slender and upright, her hands folded on her knees, betraying her uncertainty and her curiosity by her quick glances at the steering wheel in the centre of the cockpit; at the sturdy gleaming winches; and at the taut white ropes coiled round cleats.

She was about to ask Hugh a question when a man appeared in the open hatchway. Surprise flashed in his eyes when he saw her and was replaced by an expression of annoyance as he climbed into the cockpit and glanced enquiringly at Hugh, who was sitting precariously balanced on the cockpit coaming.

'Miss Penelope Jones, Tearlach. She's fully trained as a children's nanny and has a diploma to say so,' Hugh introduced her mockingly.

Tearlach Gunn, owner of the island of Torvaig, turned slowly to look again at

Penelope. He was as much a surprise to her as she was to him. Her image of a plump fatherly philanthropist had been far from the truth. This man was not much more than ten or twleve years older than herself and he must have set out on his wanderings in his mid-teens.

Not as tall as Hugh, he possessed, nevertheless, a tough muscular physique and she had the impression that he was no stranger to hard physical labour. He was wearing faded denim pants and a shirt to match, and the rough clothing emphasized the impression of tough masculinity.

As a child he must have had blond hair, thought Penelope, because his longish, untidy brown hair was still streaked with blond. The morning's sunshine had put a reddish glow in his lean square-chinned face. There was a touch of wildness to that face and the measured glance of his narrowed gleaming eyes and the calm politeness of his manner when he spoke to her only seemed to underline the wildness. The spirit of the man was as untamed as that of the original Highland chieftains from whom he was descended.

'How do you do, Miss Jones,' he said in a deep vibrant voice. 'I think a mistake has been made. I asked specifically for an older woman. I have no use for a fledgling nanny.'

Penelope returned his impersonal gaze with one which she hoped was as impersonal as his own, while inside she did a little quaking as she recognised that she was up against a formidable personality.

'I was available and I have the experience with difficult hyper-active children which was requested. Mrs. Bennet of the agency seemed to think I would be highly suitable for the job and recommended me to Mrs. Drummond,' she said evenly, thinking rather guiltily of the way in which she had pleaded with Mrs. Bennet to recommend her for the position on Torvaig, far away from London and the memories of her disastrous affair with Brian Hewitt. 'I'm quite competent,' she added coolly as he lifted his eyebrows sceptically.

'I'm not doubting your competency. I'm sure you're most efficient and that the children might benefit from being in your charge,' he replied suavely. 'My request for someone older to look after them is related to the fact that there's no other woman living in my house.'

'But surely you have a housekeeper,' said

14

Penelope, not understanding the implication behind his words.

'I have, but she doesn't live in the house. Also, should I have to go away on business, which happens often, I'd like to think I would be leaving the children with someone mature and responsible. Young women are often easily distracted from their work.'

'I am responsible,' she objected hotly. There was something about his attitude which got beneath her skin. She had a miserable feeling that this was a battle of wills she might not win. 'And I'm not a bit worried about being left alone in the house. In my last position I was often left to take full responsibility when my employers went away,' she added.

'That may have been so,' he conceded, still polite, 'but the situation at Torvaig House is different. Your last employers were a married couple. I'm a bachelor.'

Still blind to the point he was making, completely bewildered by his attitude, Penelope exploded into speech again.

'I can't see why that should prevent *you* from employing *me*.'

He looked over her head at Hugh and the curl of his mouth and the slight shrug of his shoulders conveyed, more clearly than words, his contemptuous opinion of her, and she felt her temper rising steadily.

'I'm surprised you've been able to hold a position which has put you in the care of young children,' he said in the same quietly insolent drawl. 'Your disregard for the usual proprieties, is, to say the least, reckless.'

Behind her Hugh spluttered with laughter. As she fully understood for the first time what Tearlach Gunn was implying her cheeks flushed a becoming dusky pink and she looked away from him.

'Apart from that,' he continued, 'I find you unsuitable for the job, no matter what Mrs. Bennet or my cousin, Mrs. Drummond, think.'

Her flush having subsided and her temporarily scattered wits having been collected once more she was able to glare at him, all her indignation and her disappointment revealed in her mist-blue eyes.

'Oh, this is ridiculous!' she stormed, pricked beyond endurance by his insolence. 'Just because you remember your nanny as being middle-aged and possibly dowdy, you think all nannies should be like that. I may seem too young to you, but probably I'm better trained and more adaptable than an older woman would be. If you refuse to employ me, I doubt very much if you'll find anyone else who is willing to come and live on your island, which is far away from the amenities most nannies are in a position to demand today. There aren't many of us, you know.'

Slightly unnerved by his unwavering gaze, she paused, aware that her voice was shaking. Taking a deep breath of air, she continued, determined to point out to him that he was wrong in his assumption that she had no regard for the proprieties.

'As for you thinking that I have no respect for correct moral conduct just because I have no objection to being employed by a bachelor, I'd like you to know that it never occurred to me that it might seem as if I were violating any proprieties. You must have a very low opinion of women, if you believe that because I'm willing to work in your house when no other woman lives there it should be assumed that my morals are lax. Your remark reeks of prejudice!'

Her voice shook so much that she had to stop speaking. Never before had she spoken her mind in such a way to a prospective employer. All her hopes of going to Torvaig were ruined now by her own plain speaking, and not even Hugh's softly spoken, 'Up the Joneses,' could console her.

'I never had a nanny,' said Tearlach Gunn quietly, and she remembered, rather belatedly, Hugh telling her that his cousin had grown up in one of the poorer parts of Glasgow. 'Take Miss Jones ashore and book a room for her in one of the hotels,' he went on in a brisk cold voice. 'Then buy a ticket for her journey to London.' He glanced down at Penelope again. 'The train leaves early in the morning, so make sure you're up in time to catch it. Please accept my apologies for any inconvenience caused to you for having had to travel so far north unnecessarily.'

The expression in his narrowed gleaming eyes belied his politely spoken apology. He looked as if he would have liked to have wrung her neck, she thought with a shiver. Then he turned to go down into the cabin.

'Wait, Tearlach,' said Hugh in his softly-persuasive voice. 'She's probably right. An older woman wouldn't accept the position. Why don't you give her a chance to show her mettle? After all the trouble she's taken to come this far it seems mean to send her back untried. And if you send her back, who's going to look after the bairns? I'm pretty sure Kath won't, and Swannie will throw a fit when she knows we've returned to Torvaig without anyone to relieve her.'

Tearlach's heavy shoulders stiffened and for a moment he stood perfectly still as if considering Hugh's suggestion. Then he swung round to look over Penelope's head at his cousin.

'You know the situation and what might be said,' he murmured.

'Yes, I do. But it isn't like you to be so careful of public opinion.'

'What do you mean by that?' asked Tearlach, his eyes gleaming dangerously.

'You've never seemed to mind who stayed in your house before, male or female.'

'That was before I had the responsibility of young children thrust upon me,' retorted Tearlach.

'You're taking that responsibility very seriously,' commented Hugh.

'How can I do otherwise? Avis asked me to look after them and I've never refused responsibility yet. At the moment it looks as if I'm the only relative of theirs willing to provide for them, and that means employing someone who knows about children to look after them, whether I like it or not,' replied Tearlach shortly, as if the whole business irritated him.

'You could get married and then your wife could take care of them. I know of at least one young woman who would like to marry you,' said Hugh, with a touch of flippancy.

'Then you know more than I do,' was the curt answer. 'And you're talking too much as usual.'

In the slightly uncomfortable silence which followed that sharp exchange of views, Tearlach looked at Penelope again and a faint smile curved his mouth.

'Sometimes Hugh talks sense,' he said. 'If we return to Torvaig without you, Miss Swan, who has been the children's nanny until now, is likely to have apoplexy at the thought of having to stay with them and with me a day longer than is necessary. I'm still of the opinion that you're not suitable for the job, but I could be wrong. I'm willing to give you a trial. If at the end of four weeks from now I find you can cope satisfactorily with Davy and Isa and that you don't give me any problems, I'll eat humble pie and let you stay.'

He should have been a psychologist, thought Penelope, because challenge was implicit in his offer. Without having backed down one step he had changed course. By raising a mental picture of an elderly lady struggling to deal with two lively youngsters as well as a difficult employer, he had engaged her sympathy and then had implied that she herself could do no better and would be unable to last more than a month in the position. The desire to show him that she was more than equal to the task was all-powerful, sweeping aside any other consideration, and she let it have its way.

'I accept your condition, Mr. Gunn, and you'll be eating humble pie,' she replied with a lift of her chin.

'We shall see, we shall see, Miss Jones,' he drawled, with a sudden suspicious glance at her. 'The immediate task is to relieve Miss Swan from a duty which she is finding too onerous.'

'Thank heaven you've seen sense,' said Hugh gaily, and in his turn he was regarded with suspicion by Tearlach. 'If you're really worried about the propriety of having a young single woman living in your house, I suggest you ask Mrs. Guthrie to live in. There should be enough room.'

'I'm not worried about it, but I'm pretty sure some of the islanders will be. And it's just possible Mrs. Guthrie won't agree. For all I know she might be on the side of the puritans too,' remarked Tearlach, with a wry twist to his mouth. 'Now, pull up the anchor, while I start the engine. We'll need all the power we have if we want to reach Torvaig before nightfall in this calm.'

Her immediate future settled in this surprising manner, Penelope was determined to enjoy her voyage. The idea of approaching Torvaig by sailing boat appealed to her liking for the unusual, and although she was slightly disappointed because there was no wind, she realised she could not have had a better day for seeing the scenery.

Once he had carried out the orders issued to him by Tearlach, Hugh came to sit beside her and to show her on a chart, which he brought from the cabin, the route which they would take through the Sound of Sleat into Loch Alsh, then through the narrows at the Kyle of Lochalsh to the Inner Sound, a stretch of water which

22

separated Skye from the mainland further north. They would pass the islands of Raasay and Rona and would eventually come to Torvaig, a lobster-shaped piece of land lying at the opening to one of the great sea-lochs which faced the Minch, a wide expanse of water between the Outer Hebridean Islands and the mainland.

'The Minch is as wicked a piece of water as you could wish to know when the weather is bad,' said Hugh, as he rolled up the chart. 'How about something to eat, Tearlach? It's a long time since breakfast and I'm sure Miss Jones is famished.'

'If you'd like to steer I'll make some sandwiches and something to drink,' replied Tearlach obligingly. He had steered the yacht out of the harbour and now it was moving swiftly through the water pointing north to where the Sound of Sleat narrowed as rocky spurs of land encroached upon the glittering sea.

Hugh stood up willingly and moved aft to take his place at the wheel.

'Can I help?' offered Penelope, as her new employer stepped past her on his way to the cabin.

His answer was brief to the point of rudeness.

'No.'

Then he was gone and she was glancing ruefully at Hugh.

'I suppose I shouldn't have been so outspoken,' she said.

'You both lost your cool,' he replied with a grin. 'It was like seeing two flints come together and strike sparks off each other. But you got your own way in the end.'

'Thanks to you.'

'I have my uses, and I was thinking solely of myself,' he said with that roguish twinkle in his eyes. 'Although I intend to stay a bachelor, I don't mind having a few special women friends on the side, and you could be one. But tell me, why were you so angry with him?'

'Oh, I suppose it was because he was obviously against *me*. I thought, perhaps, that he was one of those men who think that because a woman is young and presentable she must automatically be regarded as a sex object, and is good for nothing else.'

Hugh blinked his bewilderment.

'I hope you aren't one of those fervent feminists I've read about,' he said anxiously.

'Not fervent. I don't go in for bra-burning, if that's what you mean,' she said with a laugh. 'But I've always believed a woman should be recognised for her intelligence and her ability to do a job and not just for her sex-appeal.'

'That's all right, then,' said Hugh with relief. 'I think you'll find Tearlach agrees with that point of view. He's no male chauvinist, nor is he a misogynist. Quite the contrary, he enjoys the company of women, and I've a feeling there are a few females here and there in the world who were sorry when he left them behind and continued his Odyssey.'

His eyes twinkled at her as he made deliberate reference to the voyages of Ulysses and the hero's stay with various nymphs and princesses before he eventually returned to his homeland and his wife Penelope, and meeting his amused glance Penelope could not help laughing.

Sunshine, blue sea, green slopes, purple mountains. A sleek efficient yacht and a pleasant young man, with a sense of humour, for company. What more could she want? she thought, as she looked around her. Here was peace and timelessness on which it would be easy to get hooked. She wondered if the owner of

25

Torvaig knew how lucky he was to possess the yacht and live amongst such wonderful scenery.

'This is a lovely yacht,' she said to Hugh.

'It is. The hallmark of the successful man,' he replied. 'Tearlach sailed it back from the West Indies when he returned from his wanderings.'

'Alone?' she queried, wide-eyed.

'No, but he's the type who could have done a single-handed crossing of the Atlantic. He had a crew of ruffians who wanted to get back to Britain somehow and were willing to help him bring his latest acquisition here.'

'You said he was away for eighteen years. He must have been only a boy when he left.'

'He was almost sixteen. He ran away from home. He couldn't stand living in the poverty to which his father's bad management had reduced the family. He was determined to make his fortune before he came back.'

'Did he?'

'Judge for yourself,' said Hugh, waving his hand at the yacht. 'He has money and he knows how to spend it.'

'How did he make his fortune?'

26

'First of all he went to South America and, by lying about his age, managed to get work in the oil fields of Venezuela, rough tough work which pays well. Then with money in his pocket he began to speculate, buying and then selling at a profit, shares, land, anything. He's a real financial wizard, is Tearlach, and a far cry from the run-down poverty-stricken absentee landlord his father was. And all because he had the courage to kick over the traces and bolt. A school drop-out with the Midas touch.'

'You sound envious.'

'I am. I wish I had half his daring and a little of his energy. I have to admit that if he hadn't come back and had the idea of developing Torvaig into a viable economic community again, I wouldn't have been able to give up teaching in order to paint, and fish for lobsters.'

'Does he subsidise you?'

'Only to the extent of letting me have a croft for a small rent. That's one of the reasons why my mother puts up with what she calls his rough behaviour and his strange friends.'

'In what way are they strange?'

'They're not really. They're just different from the usual run of people my

27

mother prefers to know. And then some of the younger women have obviously been the fortune-seeking type.'

'Oh, I see. Then that's why there's been talk.'

Hugh flashed her a warning glance and she stopped talking and turned to see Tearlach appear at the hatchway with a plate piled high with sandwiches, two cans of beer and a mug of hot coffee. He handed her the coffee, helped himself to a handful of sandwiches and, with one of the cans of beer in his other hand, he walked off along the side-deck to the bow of the boat, without saying a word to herself or Hugh.

The sandwiches and the coffee were delicious and Penelope's opinion of her employer went up slightly. By the time she had finished them, the yacht had been sucked into a narrow strait of water and was being swept along at a rapid rate by the swirling current.

'If we didn't have enough power to beat the whirlpools we'd be helpless and would be tossed about like a cork,' explained Hugh, noting her interest. 'I've only sailed through here once or twice, and then the wind was strong and fair and we were able to keep going. But to be caught here in a calm without an engine is asking for trouble.'

Soon they had passed the whirlpools and we were in the calm waters of Loch Alsh. To the east Penelope saw five mountain peaks, soaring majestically against the sky in pastel-shaded folds of rock. The lower slopes were cleft by deep glens and at the shoreline, where they swept down to the loch, they were edged by the deep green of forests.

'The Five Sisters of Kintail,' said Hugh, 'and over there you can see the silhouette of that most romantic of castles, Eilean Donan.' He glanced towards the bow to make sure his cousin was out of earshot and added confidentially, 'You were right about the talk. Swannie has spread lurid tales about the behaviour of some of Tearlach's guests this summer, with the result that some of the older, more old-fashioned islanders will have nothing to do with him and will not work in the house. That's why he couldn't find anyone on the island to take Swannie's place.'

'Oh, I understand now why he didn't want me,' said Penelope.

'Naturally he's a little bitter about it because he's done his best for the island. By going to live there himself he's encouraged others to do so. Already many younger people have gone there to farm and fish because they know that the island has an interested owner. Ach, now, where are you going?'

Penelope had stood up and was carefully stepping out of the cockpit on to the side-deck.

'I must go and apologise for being rude to him.'

'No. If you do that he'll know I've been talking too much, and I've been reminded already today that I talk too much.'

'You're afraid of him,' accused Penelope.

'A little,' he admitted with a grin. 'I'm afraid he'll throw me off Torvaig if I don't dance to his tune.'

'That isn't very nice of you,' she reproached him. 'But no matter what you say, I must apologise. I can't work for him if I don't.'

Holding carefully to the life-lines she walked along the side-deck. As she moved forward the sound of the engine became muffled and she could hear a rushing sound, which was caused by the forefoot of the yacht as it cleaved the water. A thin spiral of tobacco smoke gave her a clue as to

30

where she would find her employer. He was sitting on the deck, in front of the cabin roof, leaning back against it. His arms were folded across his chest and between the fingers of one hand he was holding a cheroot. He was staring blankly ahead of him and there were frown lines between his eyebrows.

As she studied his profile Penelope felt her urge to apologise dying. He appeared invulnerable and completely self-contained. His mind was far away and was probably not concerned with any criticism she had thrown at him.

At that moment the yacht hit a wave, made by the wake of a fishing boat which had just passed it, and it bounced gently up and down, causing Penelope, who had not yet acquired her sea legs, to lurch forward. Wildly she grabbed at the life-line, missed it and fell right across the man sitting on the deck.

Shaken, she stared at the laid teak deck inches below her nose. Then she felt a hand on her arm.

'Are you hurt?' asked Tearlach, and she felt his legs move beneath her.

Suppressing a desire to giggle at her ridiculous position, she shook her head and

31

managed to crawl backwards off his legs. Not wishing to risk losing her balance a second time, she stayed sitting on the deck facing him, her legs curled under her.

'I'm sorry, I didn't mean to throw myself at you,' she said.

He considered her from behind a grey smoke screen before he answered.

'You mean that remark in its literal sense, I suppose,' he commented dryly, and then watched curiously as the dusky pink colour washed over her face.

'Of course,' she replied crisply. 'I was coming to apologise for losing my temper and for saying what I did.'

'You said what you felt. Why apologise for doing that? Now that I know how you feel about some subjects, I know how to deal with you,' he said coolly, enigmatically.

He raised the cheroot to his mouth and drew on it, his eyes narrowed against the bright sunlight as he looked ahead again. Not quite sure how to take his cool conception of her apology, Penelope felt she had been dismissed, and was about to stand up and make her way back to the cockpit when he surprised her by saying:

'Why are you so keen to go to Torvaig?'

'How do you know I am?' she parried.

'The disappointment expressed on your face when I told Hugh to take you ashore indicated how much you were set on getting this particular job. What is it about Torvaig which attracts you? Is Hugh the attraction?'

'Oh, no, never! My reason for wanting to go there has nothing to do with him,' she answered vehemently, annoyed that he should suspect that she and Hugh had a secret understanding of some sort. 'Nor has it anything to do with knowing you're wealthy. I'm not a fortune-seeking female. I wanted to get away from London, that's all.'

'Hugh has been talking too much again,' he murmured. 'Why did you want to leave London?'

'That's my business.'

'Then you must be on the run from something. My guess is that you're on the run from an unsuccessful love affair,' he drawled.

Unprepared for that, Penelope gasped, and he turned to give her a sardonic glance.

'Do I have to be on the run from anything?' she countered.

'If you're not hunting then you must be

escaping,' he said provocatively. 'Women are usually doing one or the other, and I can think of no other reason for someone as young and as attractive as yourself wanting to come to Torvaig.'

'I have a perfectly good reason for wanting to go to Torvaig,' she flung at him angrily. 'My grandmother on my father's side was born there. She used to tell me many stories about Torvaig and the other islands. The Happy Isles of the west, she always called them. Ever since I can remember I've wanted to come, to see the seals basking on the rocks and to watch the sunset. When the chance came in the form of work for which I'm trained, naturally I seized it.'

'And bullied the agency into recommending you even though you knew that an older woman was required,' he insinuated softly, and her eyes fell before his shrewd glance. 'What was your grandmother's maiden name?'

She could tell he was sceptical and it gave her great pleasure to look him in the eye once again and announce the old name of which her grandmother had been so proud.

'Sandison,' she said defiantly, and watched for surprise to change his expression, but not by the flicker of an eyelid or the twitch of an eyebrow did he show any emotion.

'A common enough name, hereabouts,' he conceded coolly. 'The Sandisons are a sept of the Gunn clan, as any book on the Scottish clans would inform you.'

He didn't believe her! She clenched her hands and, with a great effort, repressed a desire to go back to the cockpit and ask Hugh to alter the course of the yacht to take her back to Mallaig, because she did not think she could work for such an obdurate cynic as Tearlach Gunn.

She tried vainly to think of something to tell him about Torvaig which would convince him that her grandmother had lived there for a while, and a name sprang into her mind.

'She lived in a house called Achmore,' she persisted hopefully.

'There's no house on Torvaig of that name, although there are the ruined shells of many houses scattered here and there amongst the bracken and the heather,' he replied. Then, picking up the empty beer can from the deck beside him, he rose lazily to his feet and balanced easily on the swaying deck. 'You've thought up an ingenious reason for wishing to come to Torvaig, but I doubt the truth of your story. Like Sandison, Achmore is another name common to this part of the country. If you consulted a map before you came, which I'm quite sure you did, you'll find it mentioned often.'

He turned and made his way back to the cockpit. Penelope blinked furiously at the glitter of sunlight on the sea as the yacht nosed its way through a narrow passage of water at the Kyle of Lochalsh. A wide ferry boat crammed with cars and holidaymakers crossed in front of the yacht. Soon a small lighthouse, perched on a small rocky island, appeared on the right. A red navigation buoy loomed on the left. The land retreated on all sides and a wider expanse of water was before her, blandly blue, dotted with the dark humps of islands and edged by the majestic sweep of high mountain as it stretched north to a faint horizon.

That path of scintillating blue water led to Torvaig, and suddenly Penelope felt very close to her grandmother's spirit.

'I'm going home, Grannie,' she whispered. 'Home, beyond the sunset, to the happy isle of Torvaig, because it is home, no matter what Mr. Gunn says.'

'Do you make a habit of talking to yourself, Penelope Jones?' asked Hugh mockingly, approaching her quietly.

She glanced up at him, a little embarrassed at having been found muttering to herself.

'Not often,' she said.

He lowered himself to the deck, easing into the place which his cousin had just left, and like him, stared with narrowed eyes at the sea.

'You were cursing Tearlach, perhaps,' he suggested, with that touch of mischief which was never absent for long from his eyes and his speech. 'Did you apologise to him?'

'As much as he would let me. Is he always so sceptical?'

'What makes you ask?'

'He wouldn't believe anything I told him about my grandmother.'

'Your grandmother?' exclaimed Hugh, puzzled in his turn. 'Where does she come into the picture?'

'She was born on Torvaig and lived there until she was fourteen. She used to tell me about it. I promised her before she died that I would visit the island when I could, and look for the house where she was born, but Mr. Gunn tells me many of the houses are in ruins, and that I could have found the name of my grandmother's family in a book about the clans. He thinks I've made the whole thing up. Oh, if I wasn't so determined to reach Torvaig, now that I'm near to it, I'd ask him to put me ashore at that ferry terminus back there, and I'd find my own way back to London,' asserted Penelope, her anger with her new employer making her voice shake.

'You'd be playing right into his hands if you did,' chuckled Hugh, amused by her righteous indignation. 'He doesn't want you on Torvaig, but he's in a difficult position because he has to have someone to look after the children, and because you dared to set your will against his back there in Mallaig he's likely to make life as uncomfortable as he can for you during the next four weeks.'

'He's not my idea of a Highlander. I thought they were renowned for their good manners and hospitality,' said Penelope.

'I warned you that sometimes the roughness shows. Tearlach is not Highland-bred, nor born, and you must remember that for eighteen years he was

38

away from this country, making his way in the world alone. Of course he's hard and sometimes rude. He is also very shrewd and businesslike, but make no mistake, he can be generous and hospitable when he wants to be,' replied Hugh. 'But let's talk about something else. Tell me more about your grandmother. I'm not in the least sceptical. Perhaps I'll be able to find the house where she was born for you. I've a good knowledge of the island.'

Comforted by his offer, she told him all she knew about her grandmother's family and their reason for leaving Torvaig.

'That fits in with the general pattern of some of these islands. After the First World War many of the inhabitants left and went to live on the mainland,' he remarked. 'Although Torvaig is fairly big and has much fertile land, life was never easy in the past and cultivation was done manually. When the younger men returned from the war they were promised new houses and agricultural equipment by old Magnus Gunn, the laird of the time. But he never fulfilled his promises, and soon there were only elderly people left. Then Magnus died, and Tearlach's father inherited and did nothing.'

'Whereabouts do you live on the island?' asked Penelope.

'In a little cottage on a croft. It's on the shore of a wee cove facing the Minch. There are several crofts there. One has recently been taken by a friend of my family, Ian McTaggart. He's a silversmith. When he heard of Tearlach's aim to revive Torvaig, he jumped at the chance to come here. Like many of us he's been struggling along in a humdrum job, unable to get started in his own business through lack of capital and contacts. This summer, with Tearlach's financial support, he's been able to set up his own workshop and now he's designing and making filigree jewellery. My sister Kathleen is a jeweller too. She collects and polishes stones. She came over to Torvaig to stay with me for a holiday and went into partnership with Ian,' explained Hugh, then added with a sidelong glance in her direction, 'You and Ian have something in common. His family came originally from Torvaig too, but left to settle on the mainland.'

'Are there farms as well as crofts?' asked Penelope.

'Seven, including the Home Farm which belongs to the Gunn estate, and is managed for Tearlach by a Guthrie, another Torvaig family which has returned to the island. Dairy cattle do well. The place is green and favoured with mild weather because it's protected from the east by a great bank of mountains. In the past the mountains created a problem because they made access to the island from the mainland difficult. But Tearlach is negotiating with the local county council to have the road improved, so that dairy produce can be transported faster than it is now.'

'Does your mother live on Torvaig?' she asked. Hugh's obvious enthusiasm for life on the island was soothing her ruffled feelings. Her grandmother had not been wrong when she had described it as a lost paradise.

'Not she,' he said with a grin. 'She lives in Inverness with my father, who is a doctor. It's better if she and Tearlach don't meet often. She looks down on him because his father was no good and because his mother wasn't a Highlander, but came from somewhere in England.'

'You mentioned a car crash earlier,' said Penelope. 'Were both the children's parents killed in it?'

'Their father was killed outright. Avis

41

lingered for about a month afterwards. It was a great shock when she died as we had every hope she would survive.'

'How sad! Poor little souls,' said Penelope, sympathetically, for she knew what it was like to lose both parents at once.

'Not as poor as you would think,' replied Hugh. 'They have a wonderful place to live in and, if you stay, they're going to have a pretty nanny to look after them. Now that you know all about my relatives, let's return to yours. One way you could find out if there were really any Sandisons on Torvaig would be to visit the old graveyards. There is one near my croft. Ian is always poking about in it. Anything to do with early settlement of the island fascinates him and he fancies himself as an amateur archaeologist. You know, if you could prove that your grandmother's family once owned a croft here, you could claim it and have every right to stay on Torvaig.'

Vaguely excited by this suggestion, Penelope continued to question Hugh about the island. The yacht motored north steadily and the long island of Raasay and the small island of Rona slipped by, while the mighty Cuillins dominated the scene.

Occasionally Hugh pointed out an interesting landmark and sometimes Penelope wondered whether they should both return to the cockpit to keep the solitary man at the wheel company. But it was too pleasant sitting on the foredeck in the warm sunshine of late afternoon, listening to the bow wave as it sang its merry song. She felt she could have sat like that for ever, and began to understand why people loved to sail amongst the isles of the west.

Gradually the view changed and soon there was only the sea between them and the dark outline of the Outer Hebrides. Beneath the smooth surface of the water there was a noticeable rolling swell and it affected the motion of the yacht.

'Look,' said Hugh, pointing. 'There's Torvaig, over there.'

Penelope looked and could see only a dark shape beyond the glitter of sunlight on the sea.

'How long will it take us to get there?' she asked.

'We should reach it just before sundown. There's wind on the water. Can you see it? Maybe we'll be able to sail now.'

Rising to his feet, Hugh went back to the

cockpit presumably to tell his cousin, and realising that her pleasant time alone with him was over for the day, Penelope followed him.

When the wind reached them it was no more than a faint fanning of cooler air against her cheek and a dark shirring of the pale blue satin of the water. But it was enough for Tearlach, who ordered Hugh to set the foresail and then the sail on the small after mast. As the wind increased and thin feathery wisps of cloud streaked the western sky, the big billowing mainsail was hoisted, the engine was stopped, and the yacht bounded forward like a hound released from a leash.

Now the only noises were the sound of the water, rippling along the hull, and the occasional creaking of the masts and the boom which carried the mainsail. Sitting in the cockpit again, Penelope noticed the difference the act of sailing made to the two men.

Hugh was smiling to himself as he leaned out of the cockpit and watched the foresail. He turned to his cousin and said,

'You were right. This is the only way to approach Torvaig.'

'There's none better,' replied Tearlach.

There was a note of deep conviction in his voice which caused Penelope to look at him. His eyes were alight with excitement as he watched the mainsail, and corrected the wheel occasionally with his lean muscular hands. His legs braced against the movement of the yacht, his blond-brown hair tossed by the wind, his lean cheeks bronzed by the sun, he looked intensely alive, in love with the wind and the sea and at one with them.

Acutely disturbed by this discovery, Penelope looked away from him. The sea was building up now, under the onslaught of the steady wind. It deepened to cool greenish hollows and rose to crisp white crests. To the south of them the island had lost their warm welcoming colours and had become coolly distantly blue. Ahead, across the turbulent water towered a cliff turned golden by the light of the setting sun. On top of it a lighthouse stood, gleaming and graceful.

Rudh nan Torvaig. Torvaig Point. Penelope felt again a leap of excitement and recognition. She had never been to this place in her life before, but she knew it and had known it long before the lighthouse had been built.

She was almost home, had almost reached the island beyond the sunset.

Home! But that was how Hugh Drummond and Tearlach Gunn must regard Torvaig, and it was really much more their home than hers.

She glanced at Hugh, wanting to share her thought with him. He turned to smile at her and she smiled back. A crisp order from Tearlach interrupted their moment of silent communication. Hugh obeyed it, unwinding a rope from a winch and pulling on it. The yacht heeled suddenly. Water creamed along the teak edge of the deck. Thrilled by the burst of speed, Penelope leaned back against the coaming, tossing her hair back from her face and encountered the shrewd narrowed gaze of her empoloyer.

On meeting that searching glance her nerves quivered, but she refused to let it disconcert her and returned it frankly. Then she noticed the slightly cynical twist to the corner of his mouth. He must have noticed Hugh smiling at her. He thought she had come to Torvaig because she was a friend of Hugh's, and now, having seen them smiling at each other, he would be more than ever convinced that they had

46

known one another previously.

Annoyed to think he was still sceptical about her, she looked away over the heaving glinting sea to the island, and immediately was swept by the most alarming sensation.

She had been here before. Long ago, in the mists of time, she had sat in the company of two men and had sailed to Torvaig. But the boat had been different then. It had been open and had possessed only one short mast. The sail had been square, striped red and gold. There had been other men, sitting on benches, rowing with long oars. She had sat at the stern near the helmsman and her wrists had been bound together with a rough leathery rope.

The flashback frightened her. She shook her head to clear it and looked around. Everything was as it had been. Hugh was sprawled on the other side of the cockpit. Tearlach was steering and watching the mainsail. Glancing almost furtively at her hands she saw with relief that they were as usual, smooth-skinned and long-fingered, resting casually in her lap.

Hugh spoke suddenly, making her jump.

'The first Gunn came to Torvaig by sea. He was a Viking trader on his way back to

47

Norway with cloth and metal, as well as slaves, from Ireland. The story goes that a storm blew up and he had to take shelter in Cladach Bay, where I live now. He and his fellow seamen liked the place so well they decided to settle there. He took one of the female slaves to be his wife. It's said that her hair was as dark as a blackbird's wing and her eyes were as blue as a wee lochan on a fine day in spring.'

'That's all heady romantic stuff of the sort which appeals to Miss Jones, I'm sure,' scoffed Tearlach. His sudden grin was an attractive curving of his long upper lip over straight white teeth. 'You'll be saying next that you believe she's the reincarnation of the lass from Ireland, just because she has similar colouring, and then casting yourself in the part of the first Magnus Gunn of Torvaig. But probably she knows the story already because her grandmother, who told her so much about Torvaig, included it in her own personal tales of the Hebrides.'

His mockery was designed to needle her deliberately. Still tingling in reaction to her recent strange experience, Penelope flung a furious sparkling glance at him, hating him suddenly for his sarcasm at her expense.

'No, she didn't,' she retorted. 'But I felt

it just now before Hugh spoke.'

'Felt it?' Hugh sounded excited. He leaned forward, his tawny eyes ablaze.

'Have you ever had the feeling that you've done something before even though you *know* that you haven't in this lifetime?' she asked, guessing that he would be sympathetic and understanding.

'You mean as if you'd done it in your other time on earth?' he queried.

'That's right. Well, when I looked at Torvaig just now, I felt I'd done this before. I was in an open boat and there were men rowing it.'

'And was Hugh there, wearing a winged helmet and carrying an axe in his hand?' Tearlach's voice throbbed with scoffing laughter.

She stared at him, trying to recall the two men of whom she had been most aware in her flashback. One of them had been the steersman. The other had stood near her, hovering over her, and now, looking at Tearlach's square-chinned face, glinting eyes, derisive mouth, and sun-bleached hair, she recognised him. A description of a Viking she had once read in a history book at school flashed through her mind;

'Blond his hair and bright his cheeks
Eyes as fierce as a young serpent's.'

She was about to blurt out, 'No, but you
were,' when she realised that such an
admittance on her part would only give him
another chance to make fun of her.

'You may scoff, Tearlach,' put in Hugh
seriously, as if he'd noticed her hesitation
and wanted to help her out in an awkward
situation, 'but such flashbacks are not
uncommon. It's the inherited memory
trying to tell us something. It's possible
that Penelope really is the reincarnation of
the first Magnus Gunn's slave-wife. One of
us could be the reincarnation of him. I've
been practising yoga, which is the union of
the individual soul with the universal spirit,
for some time. It helps me to paint, and
reincarnation is a tenet of yoga. The soul
travels through several lives and has a
memory of previous lives.'

Tearlach studied his cousin's serious face
for a moment and then burst out laughing.
His laughter was a spontaneous full-
throated sound. Clearly he had no use for
fairy-tales or religious theories.

'Well, I don't practise yoga and I don't
believe in reincarnation,' he retorted

forcibly. 'And the legends about the islands were made up by the inhabitants to pass the time in the long winter, based on the truth perhaps, but exaggerated and changed so much that there's now little truth left in them. As for Miss Jones' flashback, it was nothing more than the overworking of a powerful imagination which has been fed by the romancings of her grandmother. She's imagined coming to Torvaig so often she's reached the point when she believes she's actually done it. Now that's enough of your nonsense. Go and take that mainsail down. With the wind like this we can run into An Tigh Camus under the other two sails.'

Hugh flashed a sympathetic smile in Penelope's direction and left the cockpit. Soon the white triangle of the mainsail came swishing down. He rolled it round the boom and tied it. The yacht altered course a little as Tearlach freed the foresail and it billowed out.

Looking ahead Penelope could see the rocky shore in front of the cliff. To the left of the cliff a bay was opening, a pool of crimson water reflecting the sunset. The yacht was steered towards the entrance of the bay and as the sun prepared to slip below the horizon Penelope had her first glimpse of the house where she would be living for the next four weeks. It was set back from the water at the top of a sweeping lawn and she had no memory of having seen it before.

The yacht swept round almost in a complete circle towards a red mooring buoy which bobbed on the water in the shelter of a headland which protected the bay at its north-western end. Hugh caught the buoy with a boathook and Tearlach left the wheel to run up on the foredeck to help his cousin make the mooring line fast to the kingpost on the boat, and then came back to take down the mizzen sail.

Wishing she could help with the stowing away of sails and other equipment, yet reluctant to offer help to the man who had refused her help earlier and had recently made fun of her, Penelope sat and looked about her. Dark jagged rocks protected the entrance to the bay making it almost landlocked. A curve of golden sand glinted at the foot of the green sweep of lawn in front of the house. Bare, gently rolling hills were rose-tinted by the last rays of the setting sun. The place possessed a magical quality, tranquillity plus mystery, ancient yet untouched by time, a happy isle beyond the sunset.

Yet, her future there was uncertain, complicated by the attitudes and personalities of the people she had already met and had yet to meet. Somehow during the next few weeks she had to prove her employer wrong and, in his own words, make him 'eat humble pie'.

CHAPTER TWO

In the clear light of the afterglow of the Hebridean sunset, Hugh took Penelope ashore in the dinghy, having been told to do so by a terse Tearlach, who had stayed behind to make sure his yacht was safe and ship-shape for the night.

Sitting in the bow of the dinghy, Penelope watched him moving about the deck of the yacht as it bobbed at the mooring on the swell of the evening-pale water, and she wondered whether 'things', such as boats, meant more than people to the tough, realistic owner of Torvaig.

She said as much to Hugh and he grinned at her, pushing the longish red-gold hair back from his forehead in a little boy gesture which made him seem more attractive than ever.

'Hating him, aren't you?' he shouted above the roar of the outboard engine. 'I'm not surprised. You're the type to hate him.'

'Oh. What type is that?' Penelope shouted back, intrigued by his answer.

'Independent in outlook, yet romantic at heart. Refusing to admit that any man could be your master, yet secretly nursing a hope that one day someone will turn up whom you can respect, so that you can give him all that love you have stored up inside you,' he yelled back at her. 'It's the romantic in you who hates Tearlach for his uncompromisingly realistic attitude to life. You could rip him apart, right now, for making fun of your flashback and your grandmother's stories, which obviously have meant a great deal to you. But you see he has no time for fairy-tales and legends. He's the sort of person who makes his own legend, and has done already, by living vigorously and sometimes uproariously.'

She was a little alarmed that this young man, whom she had met for the first time only a few hours ago, could read her so well. There had been a time in her life

54

when she had thought Brian Hewitt, the nephew of her employers in London who had often been a visitor at the house where she had been nanny, was the person for whom she had respect and could love.

For a while theirs had been a joyous if clandestine relationship; clandestine because of the nature of her position in his uncle's household. Then, one day, she discovered that Brian, who was a student of political science and still at university, had had similar relationships with other young women, as he had gone about making the most of permissiveness. He had thought that she was like those others and was prepared to live with him without going through the formality of marriage.

She had refused, her own inner fastidiousness dictating that she should not follow the trend. But deep depression had set in culminating in her resignation from the position in which she had been so happy and comfortable, and then in her search for another job, away from the sights and sounds of London, which had been the fascinating background for her unsuccessful love affair.

On the run from an unsuccessful love affair. Tearlach Gunn's jeer returned to mock her.

Hateful man! He had probably never known what it was like to be in love in his life!

With an effort she pushed Brian to the back of her mind. She had come to Torvaig to forget him, and she wasn't going to let her employer's jibes stop her from staying, now that she had come.

A stone jetty loomed up on her right and Hugh took the dinghy alongside it, cut the engine and jumped ashore. Making the boat fast, he helped her to get out and then took her cases.

'There's Swannie waiting on the front doorstep and wringing her hands,' said Hugh, as they walked along the jetty and on to the fine springy turf of the lawn. 'I wonder what sort of day she's had with Davy? He tends to run wild at times. The shock of his parents' death has made him nervy.'

'What about the little girl?'

'Ach, Isa is fine. A plump cushion of a bairn with a stolid down-to-earth outlook on life. But she likes to wander off and Swannie gets into a tizzy when that happens, and runs round in circles.'

Miss Swan fitted Hugh's description of a nanny exactly. She was of medium height, thin and shapeless, and was wearing a mid-calf tweed skirt and a fine wool sweater. Her hair was the colour of pale sand and her anxious blue eyes were fringed by almost white eyelashes. As soon as Hugh and Penelope were within earshot she began to complain, all the time clasping and unclasping her thin ringless hands.

'Ach, it's a terrible day I've been having with the bairns. Davy hasn't stopped whining since you left.'

'Why?' asked Hugh, as he placed two of Penelope's cases on the step in front of the porticoed front door and gazed down at the distressed nanny with an air of mild resignation.

'He wanted to go with his uncle. I did everything to pacify him, and then Isa ran away while I was seeing to him. I was fairly out of my mind with worry, wondering where she'd gone and what Mr. Gunn would say to me if she was still missing when he came back. You've been an awful long time.'

'There wasn't much wind,' replied Hugh. 'Where's Isa now?'

'They're both in bed, praise be. Your sister is reading to them. Ach, I can't think what I'd have done without her and Mr.

McTaggart today. They found Isa for me and brought her back. Miss Drummond is a dear lass, and very fond of the bairns.'

'Very fond of someone else too, I'm thinking,' said Hugh in a low voice, and winked at Penelope. She widened her eyes questioningly at him and he mouthed the word 'Tearlach' at her, over the unsuspecting Swannie's head.

'Where is Miss Jones?' asked Miss Swan, gazing at Penelope vaguely and then looking out at the bay as if expecting a person similar to herself to materialise. 'Didn't she come with you? Ach, I had a feeling she wouldn't. I told Mr. Gunn he should go by car to fetch her. Not everyone wants to sail, I said. But he wouldn't listen to me. It's quicker by boat, he said. Ach, what will I do?'

The woman wailed like a banshee, that spirit peculiar to Scots and Irish mythology whose wail portends death in the house. Afraid that she might go into hysterics, Penelope stepped forward, smiled comfortingly and introduced herself.

'I'm Penelope Jones, and I didn't mind coming by boat one little bit. In fact I enjoyed the experience. I've come to relieve you.'

For once Miss Swan was incapable of speech. She could only blink at Penelope with a flutter of pale eyelashes.

'You are never a nanny,' she exclaimed at last. 'You're too young.'

'I was the only one on Mrs. Bennet's books who would come to a place as remote as Torvaig,' replied Penelope.

'Aye, I can imagine that. It's not a place anyone in their senses would want to come. It's certainly not what I've been used to. If I'd known what sort of a man I was coming to work for I'd never have come, not even for your mother's sake, Hugh. The things your cousin has said to me don't bear repeating. And the way some of his friends, young women too, have behaved in this house—ach, it's a wonder the old lairds of Torvaig haven't turned over in their graves!'

'Now, Swannie,' cautioned Hugh, trying hard not to laugh, 'you're letting your feelings get the better of you. You'll have Miss Jones thinking my cousin is a fiend out of hell, or a twentieth-century Marquis de Sade.'

'I don't know about yon Marquis, or what he did, but I do know I've always been used to working for gentlemen who

59

know how to treat an employee. I'm sure Miss Jones is welcome to work for him, and good luck to her, for she'll be needing it,' continued the agitated little woman.

'Miss Jones is quite able to take care of herself as far as I can tell, after knowing her for only a few hours,' said Hugh comfortingly. The sound of a horn being blown carried across the water from the yacht, making a plaintive sound in the long-lingering twilight. An expression of relief passed across Hugh's face. He was obviously glad of the interruption.

'That's Tearlach wanting to be brought ashore,' he explained. 'Please take Miss Jones into the house. I expect she'd like to wash before having a meal. Leave the cases. I'll take them upstairs when I come back.'

He sprang down the steps and made his way across the lawn to the jetty. Miss Swan turned to Penelope, a rather wintry smile on her thin face.

'I'm afraid I didn't give you much of a welcome,' she said. 'Come into the house and I'll show you where your room is. I've moved out already and I'll be staying the night with a friend in the village of Strathnish, on the other side of the island.'

Suddenly realising how hungry she was,

Penelope followed Miss Swan into the house through the big panelled front door, stepping into a wide hallway with a high ceiling from which hung several carved oak Jacobean chandeliers. On the floor a priceless Persian rug glowed, red and blue, surrounded by the sheen of highly polished parquet. The walls were stark white, an excellent background for the few pieces of dark antique furniture and the numerous framed paintings and engravings.

From the hall they went up three shallow steps into a narrow passage from which doors opened into rooms she could not see. Turning left, they went down another passage to a narrow stairway, which, Penelope guessed, was the old servants' staircase. At the top of two flights of stairs there was a square landing on to which six doors opened.

'This is the attic,' explained Miss Swan. 'Give him his dues, Mr. Gunn has spared no expense in having the rooms tastefully furnished and arranged for the children. Your room is here between the children's rooms. On that side of the landing is the bathroom, the kitchen and the playroom.'

She turned the handle of a door which was painted a soft shade of green. Once in the room she closed the door firmly behind her.

The bed-sitting room allotted for her use delighted Penelope. Some antique furniture, as well as some of more functional modern design, had been entrusted to her care. The dainty walnut chest of drawers had a genuine Chippendale mirror over it and beside it, in the corner, there was a Chippendale chair of Chinese design. The simple divan bed was covered in brightly coloured folkweave material and was scattered with several cushions covered in solid jewel-like colours. Two big armchairs were set on either side of the window with a long walnut coffee table set between them. The floor was covered with fluffy pale green carpeting and folkweave curtains hung at the window.

Peering through the window, she could just make out the moorland, stretching away to a loch whose surface shone with the last pale light of evening. Beyond the loch the rugged outline of hills was carved dark against the sky.

'Do you like the room?' asked Miss Swan anxiously.

'Oh, yes, it's lovely,' said Penelope,

turning to smile at her. 'I like the old furniture particularly.'

'You'll find many other pieces like it throughout the house. It was all here mouldering away when Mr. Gunn took over the house. He let Miss Drummond have the run of the place to redecorate and refurnish it. This suite was designed for his sister and her husband and the children so that they could come and stay whenever they liked. There's no television yet, but it should be installed soon.'

'Who wants TV in a place like this with views like that?' said Penelope, waving her hand towards the window.

'I'm glad you appreciate the beauty of the place, because I'm afraid that otherwise someone as young as yourself might find living here dull, especially during the winter. Mrs. Drummond asked for a TV to be supplied because the agency told her most nannies won't take positions these days unless they can have their own private sitting room complete with television and radio. Very different from my day, not that I ever lacked for anything I wanted,' said Miss Swan with a superior sniff.

'Where were you before you came here, Miss Swan?' asked Penelope.

'Well, I'd been retired for over a year, but before that I was with the Hope-Sinclairs in Inverness. It was Mrs. Hope-Sinclair who gave my name to Mrs. Drummond when she was looking for someone to mind the bairns. Since I had known her and her family for many years I didn't mind obliging.' Miss Swan sounded as if she had conferred a great honour on Tearlach Gunn by coming to Torvaig to mind his nephew and niece.

Penelope could see now that the woman was much older than she had first thought and that she was extremely upset about something. With a surge of sympathy, knowing how uncomfortable the position of a nanny in a household could be at times, she decided she must try to put her mind at rest.

'I realise, Miss Swan, that I'm a disappointment to you. Mr. Gunn has already pointed out that he also thinks I'm too young and incapable of holding this job,' she said earnestly. 'In fact he wanted me to go back to London, but Mr. Drummond intervened.'

Surprise replaced the anxious expression on Miss Swan's face.

'Now why did Hugh do that?' she asked.

'He was thinking of you. He knows you've been unhappy here and want to leave, but he knew you couldn't go unless there was someone here to take care of the children.'

Miss Swan's face softened and tears brimmed in her eyes.

'Ach, Hugh's a good lad. It's quite true, I have been unhappy here. I'm getting too old to deal with young children and the wee laddie is difficult. He throws tantrums and cries a lot in the night. Some nights it's been three and four o'clock before I've been able to get to sleep. When I told Mr. Gunn that I thought the child should see a specialist because he has something wrong with him, he just laughed at me and said I wasn't firm enough, and that he paid me to settle the child.'

'I believe he lost his parents in an accident. Maybe he hasn't recovered from the shock of that yet,' suggested Penelope. 'Could you please tell me a little about the children's background before you go? It might help me to understand.'

Miss Swan studied the pretty face of the young woman standing before her and letting out a sigh sat down suddenly in one of the armchairs.

'I can see now that you're not what I thought you were,' she said apologetically. 'You must forgive me, Miss Jones, but you see there have been some young women staying in this house this summer whose behaviour I can only call loose. Now, I know young women are much more easy in their relationships with men today than they were when I was young, but I find it difficult to accept. Ach, it's a great load off my mind to see you're not one of those flighty pieces and that you'll have the welfare of the bairns at heart. Now, what is it you want to know?'

'I'd like to know more about the accident in which the children's parents were killed.'

'They were staying here for a wee holiday and they decided to go to the mainland and, coming back, they took one of those awful bends too fast. The car went out of control and plunged down an embankment.'

'Were the children with them?'

'No. They were left here with Mrs. Guthrie, who is the housekeeper.'

'And what were they told when their mother didn't come back for them?' asked Penelope.

'I believe Mr. Gunn told them that their

66

mother had died and wouldn't be coming any more. Ach, he didn't soften it one little bit. He has no interest in children and I think their mother made a grave mistake when she put them in his care before she died. They'd have been far better off with their father's relatives.'

'Where are they?'

'In Spain, I suppose. He was a Spaniard who worked for the Spanish Embassy in London, I believe. When you see Davy you'll see that he's no Scot. The wee lass is more like her mother, so I'm told. Their surname is Usted. It's really a lot longer than that, but Mr. Gunn said not to bother with the rest of it. Is there anything else you'd like to know?'

'No, that will do for a start. I expect Mr. Gunn will tell me anything else I want to know.'

'He might, if he's in the mood,' said Miss Swan tartly. 'You'll learn more from young Hugh or from his sister. And now I must be going. My friend from the village has been waiting for me down in the kitchen for over an hour. You'll find a cold buffet supper has been left in the dining room for you to help yourself. Mrs. Guthrie couldn't wait to see you.'

After wishing Penelope more luck, Miss Swan left. Finding her cases outside the door of the room, Penelope lugged them into the room. She decided to unpack after she had eaten.

As she washed her face and hands and combed her hair in the small bathroom she reflected quietly on everything that had happened to her that day. From the moment she had walked into Hugh Drummond at the harbourmaster's office, life had taken on a magical hue. Until then it had been blurred, almost impressionistic. Now it was sharply etched and painted in bright colours and the people who moved about her appeared larger than life-size, like those seen on a screen in a cinema.

What had made her suddenly more aware, not only of the beautiful scenery through which she had come that day but also of the people she had met? Dominating her thoughts was Hugh with his Viking good looks, his sunny smile and his soft persuasive voice. Then there was Tearlach Gunn, a close second, and never would she be able to think of him as Charles. He was cool, self-contained, *nouveau riche*, and was looked down upon not only by some of his relatives but also by the woman he had employed as nanny. He had roused her own temper so easily on the yacht that it was not difficult to imagine him upsetting the thin-skinned Miss Swan.

But there were more people for her to meet that night and as she left the room, closing the door behind her, she came face to face with a woman, a few years older than herself, who was quietly closing the door to the right.

She's beautiful, quite beautiful, thought Penelope, as she noted smoothly-braided bronze hair, fine white skin, high cheekbones and wide dark-fringed golden eyes. A tall elegant woman dressed in a long skirt made from tartan, topped by a finely-ribbed pale green sweater, which accentuated the sumptuous lines of her figure.

As usual Penelope took the initiative and spoke first as she sensed the other woman's shyness.

'I'm Penelope Jones. I've come to work here.'

The golden eyes widened even more and Penelope braced herself for the inevitable, incredulous reaction to her own appearance.

'You are never saying you're the new

nanny come to look after Davy and Isa?'
said the woman in a softly lilting voice.

'Yes, I am. You're Kathleen
Drummond, aren't you? Miss Swan told
me you were reading to David.'

'Davy,' corrected the other. 'He doesn't
like being called David. He's asleep now,
poor wee lamb. He was very upset today
because his uncle went away on the boat
without him.'

They moved towards the stairs together.
Standing back at the top of them, Penelope
let Kathleen go first. Watching the other
woman move so gracefully in her simple,
yet obviously home-made clothes, she felt
at a slight disadvantage in her trouser suit
and wished she had changed into a dress.

When they reached the lower floor and
Kathleen turned towards the wide hallway,
without saying a word, Penelope hurried
after her.

'Miss Swan said I was to go to the dining
room for my supper,' she said, 'but I'm
afraid I've no idea where it is.'

Kathleen looked over her shoulder, a
regal movement of a long white neck.

'It's the room to the right of the front
door,' she replied, and there was a touch of
condescension in her manner. 'I don't

70

suppose you'll be coming to that part of the house normally, since you have your own room in the nursery suite.'

'No, I don't suppose I shall,' murmured Penelope, as she followed the gracefully swaying figure down the three shallow steps, and thought to herself that Kathleen Drummond had none of her brother Hugh's frank friendliness.

Still in the wake of the other woman she approached the dining room and heard the sound of men's voices and laughter coming from within. The door swung wide and Tearlach Gunn came out of the room. He was still dressed in his sailing clothes and his sunburned face glowed under the forward-falling, blond-streaked hair. He held a glass half full of pale gold liquor in one hand, and as Kathleen approached him he smiled at her and said,

'I've suggested that you all stay for supper. Mrs. Guthrie has left enough to feed me and several other people.'

'Welcome home, Tearlach,' said Kathleen softly, smiling back at him. 'I'd love to stay and eat with you.'

Over Kathleen's shoulder he glanced at Penelope briefly, impersonally, then looked down again at the smiling face of his cousin.

'To receive a welcome like that when I return to Torvaig makes going away seem worthwhile,' he said, with a surprising gallantry. 'Come in.'

He turned and as Kathleen moved forward he slipped a casual arm around her shoulders to guide her onward.

Gazing at their backs Penelope thought with a grin that she had been very subtly put in her place, and followed meekly behind them.

The dining room was in keeping with the rest of the house that she had seen. It was cool, and formally furnished with an oval regency table, which was covered with a white lace tablecloth, and set with silver candelabra and cutlery.

There the formality ended, because the meal was a help-yourself buffet set out on a long sideboard at which Hugh was already helping himself to the slices of roast beef and salad. He glanced up briefly as Kathleen and Tearlach approached the buffet, and scowled at them before moving away to sit at the table. Another man was already sitting there. He had brown hair and a thick brown beard, and Penelope could only assume that he was Ian

McTaggart.

Taking her cue from the others, who completely ignored her, Penelope helped herself to food. She noted with pleasure that someone had thought to provide a pot of tea and wondered whether it was Hugh or Miss Swan who had given a thought to the new nanny. She realised that she was being allowed to eat in the dining room this evening because it was a convenient way of providing her with a necessary meal, and she was glad that Hugh and his sister and Ian McTaggart were there, for otherwise she would have been forced to eat alone with her employer. And being alone with him was something she wished to avoid.

Her plate full, she went to sit at the end of the table farthest away from him. He was lounging indolently in a beautifully-carved Jacobean chair talking to Ian who sat on his left. On the other side Kathleen sat next to her brother, who was opposite Penelope.

Looking at Hugh she had the feeling that he was deliberately avoiding her glance. Perhaps he had been warned not to associate with the new nanny, she thought. He looked rather sulky, like a small boy who had been sharply reprimanded by an adult.

Accustomed as she was to being poised between two worlds, that of the kitchen and that of the drawing room, in her position of nanny, she did not feel ill at ease as she sat slightly apart from the others. She attacked her food with good appetite, half listening to the conversation of the others.

It seemed that Ian had been digging on his land that afternoon and had found some articles buried in the soil which, he was convinced, were tools once used by Viking settlers. He was sure, he said, that the crofts where he lived were built on the site of the original Viking settlement on Torvaig and he wanted Tearlach's permission to dig further, in the hopes of discovering more artefacts and possibly the remains of a building.

Tearlach regarded the silversmith with a tolerant smile, as he listened, and then said easily,

'If it pleases you you can dig up the whole of your land searching for tools and walls. I can't see that you'll offend anyone as long as you keep within your own boundaries. But you won't get much other work done while you're doing that sort of digging. What else do you hope to find?'

'There may be the remains of a Viking house such as the ones which have been excavated at Borsay in the Orkney Islands and at Jarlshof in the Shetlands,' replied Ian in his deep sing-song voice.

'And supposing there is, what good will that do any of us?' asked the practical, realistic Tearlach.

'It will prove once and for all that the first settlers on Torvaig were Vikings, as the legend tells us,' put in Hugh, shaking off his sulks and joining in the conversation enthusiastically. 'I'll help with the digging, Ian. I once helped with a dig at Stirling. We found some Roman nails.'

'Do you share all this preoccupation with the past of Torvaig, Kathleen?' drawled Tearlach. 'Perhaps you have visions, like our new nanny, Miss Jones. This afternoon she "felt", so she says, that she had sailed across the sea to Torvaig in a Viking ship.'

There was no mistaking the jeer in his voice. Penelope's head jerked up in reaction and she sent an angry glance in his direction, while her cheeks went pink as she realised that both Ian and Kathleen had turned to stare curiously at her.

Tearlach returned her glare coolly, a faintly mocking smile hovering about his mouth, and she knew suddenly and instinctively that the battle between them was joined. He was going to make her life as uncomfortable as he could for the next four weeks, using every weapon available to him.

Kathleen laughed, a delicious musical sound.

'How silly of Miss Jones,' she remarked. 'No, I'm not at all fascinated by the past. I'm strictly a woman of the present, gathering rosebuds while I may.'

Tearlach slanted her a narrowed speculative glance while he selected a cheroot.

'And what does that mean?' he murmured.

'It means I'm not going to waste any time delving into the past when the present is all too brief and I have so much living to do,' replied Kathleen, and it seemed to Penelope that there was subtle invitation in the way the woman looked at Tearlach. 'Don't you know the poem by Robert Herrick in which he advised young virgins to make good use of their time?'

'No. I haven't read much poetry,' said Tearlach, with a grin. 'I've been too busy living. How does it go?'

'Like this:

Gather ye rosebuds while ye may,
Old Time is still a-flying:
And this same flower that smiles today,
Tomorrow will be dying.'

quoted Kathleen softly, smiling at him.

'An interesting philosophy, much like my own,' said Tearlach, and again his glance lingered assessingly on his cousin's lovely face, which seemed to gleam with a radiance of its own.

Gritting her teeth so as not to show how irritated she was by Kathleen's amusement at her expense, Penelope drank her tea. The warm sweet liquid was comforting as ever. As she replaced the cup on the saucer her eyes encountered those of Ian McTaggart. He was gazing thoughtfully at her. He looked away first, obviously shy.

The conversation continued on more general terms and Penelope closed her ears to it, finished her meal and decided to have another cup of tea. At the sideboard she poured milk into her cup and was about to add sugar when a lean hand appeared and took the sugar bowl from her. She looked up into eyes which were narrowed against a spiral of grey smoke rising from a cheroot. Tearlach raised a hand and removed the cheroot from his mouth to speak to her with smooth politeness.

'You must be tired after your journey, Miss Jones.'

'No, not at all, thank you, Mr. Gunn,' she replied cheerfully, and turned to pick up the teapot. But the same lean hand which had taken the sugar bowl was there again, setting the pot just beyond her reach.

'I believe Miss Swan showed you to your room and that Hugh has taken your luggage up there,' he said.

'Yes. The room is very pleasant,' she replied, refusing to be disconcerted.

'I'm glad you think so. Davy wakes up in the night crying for his mother, sometimes, and Isa is an early riser, so I advise you to go to bed early. Sleep seems to be an essential part of a nanny's life if she is to keep up and give the right amount of attention to such active youngsters,' he added, still smooth. 'Good night, Miss Jones.'

He was really telling her that she was no longer welcome in the dining room. He had allowed her to take a meal with him and his guests, but that did not entitle her to linger and listen to the conversation.

Penelope felt again the faint stirring of rebellion as her gaze clashed with his. She longed to treat him with the smooth insolence he showed to her. Then she remembered he had said she would not last a month in this job. She must not play into his hands by giving him the chance to dismiss her, so she bowed her head and murmured meekly, 'Good night, Mr. Gunn.'

Going across to the chair she had sat in, she collected her handbag and walked to the door. As she went her eyes met those of Kathleen, who had obviously been very interested in the short verbal exchange at the sideboard. Mockery gleamed in the clear golden eyes before they turned away to look at Ian, who was talking.

Infuriated by that mockery, Penelope tilted her chin and said loudly,

'Good night, everyone,' then turning on her heel, she marched out of the room.

She had reached the nursery before she had calmed down. As she closed the door of her room and switched on the light she heard the unmistakable sound of a child sobbing. Instantly she forgot her own bruised feelings. The sound was coming from the right, from the room where Davy slept.

Going to the communicating door, she opened it quietly and stepped into the other room. It was full of shadows cast by the night light which glowed on the chest of drawers. She could see quite clearly the small bed in which a figure was hunched under the clothes.

She went over and sat on the side of the bed. Speaking his name softly, she touched the little boy. He stopped sobbing and raised his head to look at her. She could see that he was thin and that he had a mop of dark hair and great dark eyes.

'Hello,' she said. 'I'm your new nanny.'

'Go away!' he howled, in disappointment. 'Don't want you! Want Uncle Tear. Kathy said she would ask him to come and see me and he hasn't come. Go away! Don't want new nanny!'

Sobs shook him afresh, as he buried his head in the pillow, and for the next half-hour Penelope's training and ingenuity were put to the test as she tried every method she could think of to calm him. But nothing worked and eventually she rose quietly to her feet and left the room.

She intended to undress and go to bed, thinking that the child's crying would subside and he would fall asleep through sheer exhaustion. Although it went against the grain to allow that to happen, it was also quite obvious that there was nothing that a stranger like herself could do to make up for the neglect of the child by his uncle. But standing there listening to the sobs, she realised she could not rest either, knowing that a child was disturbed. She had to take action, and the only action left to her was to go and find Tearlach Gunn and tell him his nephew wanted to see him.

Leaving her room to go downstairs, she wondered if Kathleen Drummond had kept her promise and had told Tearlach that he was needed by Davy. Or had the lovely Highlander conveniently forgotten to tell him because she had not wanted to share the attention he gave to her with a small motherless boy?

There was certainly something special going between the forceful, arrogant owner of Torvaig and his beautiful cousin, thought Penelope, and, if ever she had seen two of a kind together, she had seen them tonight, both of them confident in their ability to attract the opposite sex, both intent on grasping any pleasure the present offered, two believers in the cult of Now.

The stairs were dark and the house was quiet. As she reached the hall she realised she had no idea where to look for her employer. For all she knew he could have gone out with his supper guests to walk in the perfect moonlit night.

Temporarily nonplussed, she stood quietly in the middle of the hall listening. There was no sound from the dining room although the light still blazed in there. On the other side of the hall a door stood partially open revealing the moon-dappled darkness of another room.

'In here, Miss Jones.'

The sound of Tearlach's voice from behind her made her jump. Swinging round, she saw another door wide open. She advanced towards it and on entering saw him lounging in a big leather chair behind a wide desk. His feet were on the desk and he was holding a sheaf of papers in his hand.

'I gather you're looking for me,' he said coolly.

'Yes. Davy keeps crying and won't go to sleep.'

His thick dark eyebrows rose a fraction.

82

'Defeated already, Miss Jones?' he jeered.

'No,' she snapped. 'Miss Drummond promised him that she would tell you he wanted to see you before he went to sleep, and nothing else will satisfy him. He was sobbing when I went to my room, and although I've tried every way I can think of to comfort him, he still insists on seeing you.'

'And you, judging by the disgust in your voice and the expression on your face, are thinking I'm a monster for not having been to see him,' he remarked dryly. He swung his feet down from the desk, threw the papers down, stood up and came towards her. 'Kathleen didn't tell me,' he said.

'Probably she had other and more interesting things to tell you,' replied Penelope stiffly. 'Little children are often forgotten when they're out of sight and there are more important people around on whom one wants to make an impression. Will you come now and see Davy?'

'Yes, I will. But first I should like to warn you, Miss Jones, that catty remarks on your part about my guests are not welcome,' he said freezingly. 'You will keep your opinion of them to yourself in

83

future.'

Remembering rather belatedly that she must not give him any chance to sack her, she once more bowed her head with reluctant meekness, her long dark eyelashes fanning out on her cheeks as they covered her eyes.

'Yes, Mr. Gunn,' she muttered.

'Meekness suits you, Miss Jones,' he said softly. 'Perhaps if you remember that you will not be so tempted to twist the lion's tail.'

He turned and walked out of the room. Slightly disconcerted by his last remark, Penelope followed, thinking that with his shaggy golden-brown hair, deceptively sleepy eyes and big bulky shoulders he reminded her of a lion.

He took the narrow stairs two at a time and by the time she arrived, slightly out of breath, he was sitting on Davy's bed talking to him. He glanced at her when she entered the room and, pausing in what he was saying, jerked his head in the direction of her room. Taking that as a hint that he did not want an audience while he talked to the boy, she retreated.

In her room she stood by the window looking out at the moonlit countryside wondering what she should do next. Should she go to bed or should she stay and wait for her employer to tell her he had finished talking to his nephew? She was still rather surprised that he had come so willingly to talk to the little boy. Going by Miss Swan's opinion of him, she had expected to have had a hard time persuading him to leave his papers to give of his time to the child. He was really rather a disconcerting person and he had no hesitation in speaking his mind, as his reprimand concerning her remark about Kathleen had shown. Of course, she should never have made such a remark in the first place. In doing so she had acted completely out of character. She knew full well that a person in her position had no right to make remarks about her employer's guests.

But then she had acted peculiarly all day, almost as if she *were* another person. The reincarnation of the first Magnus Gunn's slave wife, perhaps?

Irritated by her wayward thoughts, she tiptoed to the communicating door and opened it. The room beyond was quiet except for the sound of a child's breathing, occasionally interrupted by sobs. There was no one sitting on the bed. Davy was asleep and Tearlach had gone back to his study.

With a sigh Penelope turned back to her own room leaving the door slightly ajar. She went over to the other communicating door which she assumed led to Isa's room. In there a night light also glowed, revealing the little girl comfortably asleep in her cot, her plump cheeks rosy and her gold-streaked brown hair fanned out on the pillow.

Satisfied that her new charges were settled for the night, Penelope unpacked a few articles of clothing ready for the next day and prepared for bed. Once again she was aware of the silence, not only in the house, but also outside. Here, on Torvaig there was no noisy traffic to pollute the fresh air which wafted in through the open window.

Contentedly she snuggled down in the comfortable bed. It was not until she was drifting off to sleep that she remembered that, apart from the two children, there were only herself and Tearlach Gunn in the house that night.

The next day, her first in Torvaig House, was extremely tiring and exacting, partly because, being conscientious about her work, she made it so and partly because of the demands made upon her by the two children.

As Tearlach had pointed out, the two-year-old Isa was an early riser. She was on the go in her room from six o'clock onwards, chattering to herself as she sat in her cot. Listening to the little girl's voice, Penelope decided that she might as well get up and make her acquaintance before Davy awoke. If he had behaviour problems it was possible he would require a great deal of attention and then the little girl would suffer. Time must be set aside during the day for Isa to receive attention on her own.

Fortunately Isa had a happy disposition and accepted without question her new nanny, showing off her teddy bear and the other soft toys she had taken to bed with her. She showed a certain amount of feminine independence by insisting on dressing herself in a T-shirt and dungaree-style pants, socks and shoes, but allowed Penelope to brush her long, sunbleached brown hair and tie it up with a red ribbon.

In the small kitchen Penelope found everything she required to cook simple meals, including well-stocked cupboards and a small refrigerator. Under the window there was a table and four chairs where meals could be taken.

Isa chattered all the time, repeating herself many times in the manner of a two-year-old while Penelope prepared cereal for the little girl, to be followed by a soft-boiled egg, and drank tea and ate toast for her own breakfast.

They were still eating when Davy burst into the room. He was still wearing his pyjamas. He snatched Isa's orange juice from her and poured it all over the table and then threw the plastic mug across the room, in a fine display of jealousy. His black eyes glowing, he began to stamp round the room, screaming at the top of his voice.

Thrown a little off balance by this startling behaviour, Penelope stared at him for a moment, wondering if he were deranged. Then she caught his sidelong glance in her direction and knew it was a deliberate attempt on his part to upset her as, presumably, he had been able to upset Miss Swan.

Hiding a grin with a severe frown, she looked at him coldly and told him sharply to stop screaming and to go to his room and dress. He took not the slightest notice of her, so she grabbed him the next time he stamped past her, picked him up, smacked his bottom lightly, carried him to his room and, setting him down just inside the door, left him there with a final sharp instruction to get dressed or he wouldn't have any breakfast.

Glaring at her with rather surprised black eyes, he retaliated by banging the door closed. Ignoring his action, Penelope began to mop up the mess he had made. She was still wiping juice from the table, while Isa reiterated over and over again, 'Davy naughty boy, Davy naughty boy,' when there was a knock at the door. It opened and a small plump woman whose black hair was snatched up into a bun on top of her head, and who was wearing an apron over her flowered print dress, came into the room and introduced herself as Bessie Guthrie, the housekeeper.

'Ach, you are young, an' no mistake. I can see now what himself is getting at,' she said, going straight to the reason for her visit. Behind her glasses her brown eyes twinkled as she sized up the young woman who was carefully wiping the table. 'From London too, I've been told. Then you should be able to take care of yourself, well enough.'

'Have done most of my life,' replied Penelope with a grin.

'Aye, I can see there's no nonsense about you and that you're here to do a job—which is more than I could be saying for the last nanny we had. We weren't good enough for her and Mr. Gunn hadn't been to the right schools and didn't have the sort of manners she was used to,' said Mrs. Guthrie, mimicking Miss Swan's soft complaining voice. Then peering over her glasses at Penelope she added in her own voice, 'Spread tales about him, she did, and there are some folks on this island who believed her, just because yon man is a wee bit different from the usual run of lairds Torvaig has had!'

'Oh. How is he different?' asked Penelope.

'Well, for one thing he doesn't think of the place just as his country estate, a place to bring his friends to hunt and fish, as the others did. He's made it his home. Then he holds to the principle that charity with no strings attached leads to apathy, so he only offers aid to those who are willing to help themselves with the result the farms are farmed properly and the crofts are being worked. The owners know that if they produce they'll receive aid in the way of new equipment and buildings,' asserted the plump woman.

'Since you have such a high opinion of Mr. Gunn, I suppose you are willing to agree to his request that you should come and live in while I'm here, to prevent any further damage to his reputation,' said Penelope, untying Isa's bib and lifting her down from her chair.

'Ach, well now, it isn't as easy as all that. You see Alec and I have our own wee cottage on the estate which we like well enough, and it's really up to him to decide. A man likes his own fireside, especially when he's getting older, and he may not take kindly to moving into the two rooms downstairs which Mr. Gunn says we could have,' explained Mrs. Guthrie.

Presuming that Alec was Mrs. Guthrie's husband, Penelope asked if he worked on the estate.

'Aye, he's the head gardener. Gardening is his love and his work, and always has been,' said the housekeeper. 'We were over on the mainland on the Falkland estate, but when Jimmy, my eldest son, came here to manage the Home Farm and learned that

Mr. Gunn wanted someone to rescue the garden of the house from the wilderness it had become, Alec came right over and asked for the job. He was born here on the island, you see, and lived here until he was called up into the army during the last war. He didn't come back because there was nothing to come back to, but all the years I've known him he's wanted to come back.'

'I wonder if he ever knew anyone called Sandison on Torvaig?' asked Penelope.

'You can ask him yourself, lass, when he comes in for his elevenses. Come into the kitchen then and have something yourself. Bring the bairns with you. They're as much at home there now as they are anywhere because Miss Hoity-Toity Swan often used to leave them with me. I'd like Alec to meet you, anyway, because then he'll understand the need for us to move into the house to stop the tongues from wagging, and he might be more agreeable to the idea.'

Pleased and relieved to find Mrs. Guthrie was a friendly sensible woman, Penelope promised she would go down later to have a cup of tea with the head gardener, and the housekeeper left the room. As soon as she had gone Penelope went to Davy's room. He was lying on his bed sobbing again.

'Go away!' he shouted at her. 'Don't want you. Want Uncle Tear.'

'Well, you can't have him, so you'll have to put up with me,' she replied cheerfully.

He was really a very beautiful child, she thought, with his black waving hair, golden skin, and elegantly chiselled features, but he required firm handling and she guessed he got it from his uncle and responded to it, so she intended to use the same methods. It was just possible that Miss Swan had found him exhausting and demanding because she had allowed her compassion for him to get out of hand, and had consequently been too soft with him. Davy, she decided, would use his very obvious masculine charm to get his own way and then, when he saw that failing, would resort to tempers and tantrums.

It was a fight to make him sit down and eat his breakfast, but it was the first fight and Penelope was determined to win it. After that he seemed more disposed to do as she asked and occasionally gave her the benefit of his brilliant smile. Like most four-year-olds, he wanted to do much more than he was capable of and possessed a great deal of energy which had to be directed.

At eleven o'clock Penelope found she was quite glad to take advantage of Mrs. Guthrie's suggestion and go down to the kitchen for a cup of tea.

As she entered the big room a short stocky man in his middle fifties who had a shock of grizzled dark hair stood up politely and held out a square, rough-skinned, work-gnarled hand to her.

'I'm thinking you're the lassie from London,' he said, in a lilting Hebridean drawl. 'I'm Alec Guthrie.'

His shy smile seemed to split his long face in two and his Celtic blue eyes twinkled under the dark bushy eyebrows, which threatened to hide them from view.

'Sit down, Miss Jones,' said Mrs. Guthrie, 'and tell me how you like your tea. Here, put the wee lassie on this stool. She'll be liking a glass of milk and a biscuit, I shouldn't wonder, and the same for Davy. Ach, there he goes to his favourite place.'

As Alec Guthrie sat down again Davy went straight to him and climbed up on to his knees, happily sure of his welcome. He placed his two small hands around Alec's big mug of tea and, with some help, lifted it to his mouth and took a sip of tea.

'Now you can be asking your question

94

about the Sandison family,' prompted Mrs. Guthrie, as she passed a cup of tea to Penelope. 'Did you say they lived on Torvaig at one time?'

'Yes, my grandmother was a Sandison and she was born here, but her father decided to leave the island when she was in her teens and she went with him.'

'He would be Hector Sandison,' said Alec. 'The Sandisons held crofts over Cladach way for many generations. Your grandmother's father was a lively, rebellious sort of man, but intelligent too. He led several deputations of crofters to the old laird, Magnus, to try and persuade him to make improvements to the island, by helping the crofters to buy modern farm machinery and by re-allocating some of the land. But Magnus wouldn't listen. He preferred to think of the whole of Torvaig as his country estate and he even encouraged islanders to leave, so that he could have the place to himself and his hunting and fishing friends. In disgust Hector Sandison left and went to the south of England to work. So your grandmother was Heather Sandison? She was a friend of my mother's. Have you told Mr. Gunn?'

'Yes, but he didn't believe me. I'm afraid

95

he's very suspicious of me because I'm not his idea of a nanny.'

Alec Guthrie chuckled, a warm infectious sound.

'I can't say you're my idea of a nanny either. I can see why he wants Bessie and me to live in the house here. When it gets round the island that there's a pretty young woman living at the big house there'll be a great blethering.' He turned and looked at his wife. 'When did you say he wanted to know our decision?'

'By this afternoon. Ach, having the care of these bairns put upon him has put him in a difficult position, there's no doubt of that,' sighed Mrs. Guthrie. 'Before, he didn't need a housekeeper who lived in and that suited him and us fine. And it was all right when Miss Swan was here because with her being older, no one cast aspersions on either her or him.'

'I'm thinking that Miss Swan made his position difficult,' mused Alec, staring down into his mug. 'If she hadn't carried tales about that young woman who was staying in the house earlier this summer, he wouldn't be worrying about what might be said about Miss Jones here.'

'Aye, but it's himself he's protecting

too,' said Mrs. Guthrie.

'Then what do you think we should do?' asked her husband.

'You know how I feel about Tearlach Gunn. I'd do anything to help him because of what he's done for the people of Torvaig.'

'I thought that would be the way of it,' said Alec with a grin and a wink in Penelope's direction. 'Then you'd better be telling him we'll do as he asks and we'll start moving in today. I daresay young Wilson who has just come to work on the Home Farm, will be glad to move into our cottage while he's waiting for his own to be built. He and his wife are lodging with the Browns in the village, but she's expecting a bairn and would be glad to be on her own.'

The problem of providing her (or was it her employer?) with a chaperone solved, Penelope spent the rest of the morning going for a walk with the children. It was not a very long walk, only down to the jetty and back. Then they had lunch in the kitchenette and Isa was put down for her afternoon's rest. For the next hour Penelope spent the time getting to know Davy better. She discovered that he knew his alphabet and some numbers and that he had several games using letters and numbers which he could play with her. He also enjoyed doing simple jig-saw puzzles of which he had quite a collection.

When Isa awoke they went for another walk and this time managed to walk a little further along the shore as they tossed pebbles into the calm water of the bay. As she returned slowly to the house holding the hands of both children, Penelope realised that she was going to be severely restricted as to movement on the island because neither of the children could walk very far. The chances of her exploring the place were limited while she had to stay with them. Some time in the near future, when she felt more secure, she would have to ask her employer about free time. He could not expect her to stay with the children all day and every day. Even nannies were entitled to a few hours off to attend to their own needs.

A tug at her right hand made her look down. Davy was doing his best to escape from her grasp.

'Uncle Tear, Uncle Tear!' he shrieked in his piercingly shrill voice. 'Wait for me!'

Looking towards the house she saw a sleek black car parked on the driveway.

Tearlach Gunn was just about to open a door and get into it. He turned when he heard his name being called.

'Hello, Davy,' he said, and leaving the car, came towards them. He was dressed in a dark brown tweed sports jacket and fawn-coloured trousers. A green paisley patterned neckerchief was knotted round his neck inside the open collar of his fawn-coloured shirt. The sunburn of the day before had toned down to a uniform bronze colour, emphasizing the clear-cut angles of his face and contrasting attractively with his blond-streaked hair and the whiteness of his teeth when he smiled at Davy and Isa. The full force of his aggressive masculinity hit Penelope hard, putting her on the defensive immediately.

'Look what I've found, Uncle Tear,' said Davy, encouraged by the smile and holding up a shell he had found.

'Flowers, pink flowers, pretty flowers,' sang Isa, holding up a posy of sea pinks she had gathered. 'Uncle have pink flowers.'

'Thank you, Isa,' he said gravely, taking the proffered posy, and then, to Penelope's surprise, he bent and picked the little girl up in his arms. Holding her high against his shoulder, he said. 'How do you like your

99

new nanny?'

'Nice nanny, pretty nanny,' said Isa magnanimously, leaning forward to pat Penelope's smooth shining hair with a chubby hand.

'How about you, Davy?' asked Tearlach. 'Miss Jones suit you as a nanny?'

'She's all right,' conceded Davy. 'I want to go for a ride in your car. Please, Uncle Tear.'

An impatient frown twitched Tearlach's eyebrows together and he glanced at his wrist watch. Sensing his reluctance to give in to the little boy's request, Penelope supposed this was a time when she should step in and remove the children from his sight. But that faint flutter of rebellion which she always felt when in the presence of this self-confident man kept her quiet and stationary. Let him get out of his predicament himself, she thought.

'Not just now, Davy,' said Tearlach smoothly, allowing Isa to slide to the ground. Immediately both children burst into tears.

'It's the least you could do for them,' Penelope found herself hissing at him.

'And give you a much-needed rest from them, I suppose,' he retorted. 'Oh, no. I may have helped to settle Davy for you last night, but don't count on me to relieve you from your work by taking him for drives round the island.'

'Unlike you, I'm not thinking of myself all the time,' she retaliated, casting caution aside. 'I'm thinking of him. You must know how he adores you. You are his mother's brother and so you represent security to him in her place. Is it any wonder he wants to be with you more than with me? He hardly knows me yet. Don't you realise you're in a position to make or break that boy's faith in others?'

That unpleasant expression was back in his eyes and she stepped back, afraid that he might do what his eyes threatened, wring her neck. But the wild look faded and he laughed, a good-humoured sound. Hands on his hips, he looked down at her almost tolerantly, while he ordered Davy and Isa to be quiet.

'In exchanging Miss Swan for you I seem to have exchanged a twitterer for a termagant,' he scoffed. 'Where did you learn to brawl with your employer, Penelope Jones? It isn't done, you know, if you want to keep your job. Don't forget, you're walking a tight-rope, here at Torvaig

101

House. One false move and you fall, at the end of four weeks.'

'That doesn't mean I'm going to sit by and watch you destroy a child's faith in you,' she answered. 'You have the care of these children and it's up to you to take the place of their father. Giving them toys and every comfort isn't enough. You have to give something of yourself and your time.'

The humour fled from his face, leaving it hard and cold. She had the impression she had touched a sensitive spot.

'Quite finished?' he asked harshly. Taking herself in hand, she nodded dumbly. 'Then I shall do as Davy asks. I'll take him and Isa for a drive. But don't think you're going to have some free time. You can sit in the back of the car with Isa and keep an eye on her. We'll go to the ferry, and that way it's just possible I'll be able to kill two birds with one stone, without putting myself to too much inconvenience. Come on, Davy lad, in you get.'

The little boy needed no second bidding and scrambled into the front seat beside the driver's when Tearlach opened the door for him.

Slightly dubious about her employer's

sudden change of mind, Penelope helped Isa climb into the back seat of the car and sat down beside her, keeping behind Tearlach's broad shoulders so that he could not see her without having to turn right around.

Yet in spite of her turbulent state of mind she could not help being excited at this first opportunity to see more of the island.

From the front of the house they followed a winding road through the mixed woodland which lay to the east of the house. Then leaving the shadow of the trees they joined another wider road which curved over the moorland round the head of the small loch which Penelope could see from her bedroom window.

Striking across the wild moorland country, where the feathery fronds of emerald bracken alternated with a purplish haze created by heather just coming into bloom, the road twisted in a series of hairpin bends between drystone walls, rising gradually to the top of the rocky ridge of hills which formed the spine of the island.

Once over that ridge it began to descend again to flatter land where lush meadows were dotted with thoroughbred dairy cattle whose golden coats glistened in the sunlight. A white-gabled farmhouse appeared and a man driving a red tractor along the road raised his hand in greeting as they passed. Tearlach responded with a wave of his hand and, after a slight hesitation, Davy gravely imitated him with a slow, unconsciously regal salute, just like a young prince, thought Penelope with a grin.

The road wound eastwards towards the coast, past fields where barley and oats waved under the summer wind, past the ruins of old cottages overgrown with tall grasses amongst which red poppies blazed.

Her annoyance with Tearlach forgotten, her interest in the island revived by all she could see, Penelope asked a question.

'How big is Torvaig?'

'I thought you'd know. Didn't your grandmother tell you?' was the mocking reply, making her grit her teeth and clench her hands.

'Grandmother? What's that?' asked Davy, before she could think of a retort.

'Who, not what,' corrected Tearlach lazily. 'Your nanny has a grandmother, so she says. Why not ask her?'

Davy leaned over the back of his seat to

gaze at Penelope with intelligent dark eyes.

'What's grandmother?' he demanded.

Swallowing the acid remark which she had found to fling at her employer, she said instead, 'The mother of your mother or father. You usually have two.' Satisfied with her answer, Davy slid back into his seat.

'Do I have a grandmother?' he asked Tearlach.

'Yes, you have one.'

'Where is she?'

'In Spain. She's your daddy's mother.'

'I want to see her.'

'Perhaps one day you will.'

'I want to see her now,' stated Davy with his usual determination to get his own way.

'Can't be done, Davy,' replied Tearlach cheerfully. 'Look over there. You can see the ferry coming across from the mainland.'

He was really very good with the boy, thought Penelope, as she also looked and saw sunlight glinting on the dimpling blue water of a narrow strait. Beyond the water, rolling moorland, purple and black, sloped upwards to cliffs of rock with pointed peaks, silvery grey and rose, cleft by deep shadowed gullies.

Soon they were passing down a village street, past a row of semi-detached houses of modern design, past the low squat original cottages. Flowers blazed in neatly-kept gardens. Some children ran by, laughing and shouting. They waved to the black car and received the usual careless wave from Tearlach and the more sedate salute from Davy.

Then they were turning down a rough road towards the ferry terminus. There was no other car waiting, but there was one person standing alone, a tall woman whose bronze-coloured hair glowed. She was wearing a simple green dress and round her shoulders was draped a wide plaid of scarlet and green tartan.

There was only one woman she knew who could wear a plaid like that in this day and age, thought Penelope, as she watched Kathleen Drummond turn at the sound of the car and wave. There was no doubt that she was expecting Tearlach, and she must be the reason why he had been reluctant to take his nephew for a drive.

CHAPTER THREE

Tearlach did not take the car right down to where the ferry docked, but parked off the road to the slipway and sat watching the ferry approach. He did not seem to have seen Kathleen, or, if he had, he did not acknowledge her wave, and when she saw that he had company in the car, Kathleen turned away and also watched the ferry.

'I'd no idea the island was so near to the mainland,' exclaimed Penelope.

Tearlach turned in his seat and slanted her a sardonic glance over his shoulder.

'Something else your grandmother didn't tell you?' he mocked. 'Distances are deceptive. The strait is five miles wide, wide enough to have made transporting goods and people a problem in the past. The road through the mountains on the other side is in poor shape and takes only single line traffic. It was on that road that the accident took place in which Davy's father was killed and my sister was fatally hurt.'

Penelope felt she should show some sympathy, so she said softly, 'It must have been very sad for you when she died after lingering so long.'

A strangely dour expression flitted across his face making him look older.

'If she'd lived she would have been no more than a vegetable,' he murmured, then added more crisply, 'Don't waste too much sympathy on me, Miss Jones. I hardly knew my sister. She wasn't much older than Davy is now when I left home. My biggest regret concerning her untimely death is that it has left me in charge of two young children.'

While Penelope was recovering from the effect of this abrupt, hard speech, he opened the door and stepped out of the car. Davy scrambled after him. As soon as she saw Davy go, Isa wanted to get out too, and soon they were all standing beside the car watching the ferry dock.

A small green car, very new and very shiny, trundled off the ferry. It was driven by a young man who brought it to a stop just ahead of the black car, opened the door and stepped out.

'Everything all right, Donald?' asked Tearlach, who began to walk round the Mini, examining it carefully.

'Fine, just fine. I had no trouble at all,'

replied the young man.

'Good. Give me the keys.'

Donald handed over the keys and glanced curiously at Penelope as Tearlach walked back to her and said brusquely, 'Hold out your hand, Miss Jones.'

Releasing Isa's hand, she held out her right hand obediently, and he dropped the car keys into it.

'It's for your use,' he said. 'Like the TV, it was supposed to be here before you arrived, but there was some difficulty about delivery. It's important to me that you and the children should be as independent as possible. Now Davy can have as many rides as he likes without having to ask me and you won't feel so restricted.'

She stared in amazement at the keys in her hand. He said another few words to the interested Donald, called good-bye to the children, swung behind the wheel of the black car and let it drift slowly down to the ferry. He stopped beside Kathleen, who put her case on the back seat and sat down beside Tearlach, before the black car moved forward on to the ferry. Still startled by her employer's latest move, Penelope put the excited children into the back seat of the little two-door car and then offered a lift to the young man who had driven it up from the factory. He turned out to be Donald Lang, a crofter who was also a motor mechanic and who looked after the agricultural machinery which was used on the farms. He accepted a lift as far as Torvaig House, where he said he had left his own van. On the way to the house he told her that he and his wife Molly had their croft on the shores of Cladach Bay, where Hugh Drummond also lived, and invited her to call in any time she was over that way.

In the days that followed Penelope found the green Mini car a great help and wished that she had been able to show her appreciation to her employer for his thoughtfulness in providing it for her use. That was not possible, however, because, as Mrs. Guthrie informed her, having learned that the Guthries had agreed to live in the big house, Tearlach had gone to the mainland on business and would not be back until the following week, and then he would be bringing guests with him.

Penelope soon worked out a routine for herself and the children. She kept to it closely, knowing that consistency of behaviour on her part would develop a sense of security in them. She took them for drives every day to a different part of the island, and discovered that it was much bigger than she had realised. Its scenery varied considerably. In the north end there was a high flat-topped mountain, Ben Luran, on which it was said the witches used to dance on May Day eve and on Hallowe'en, and the whole of the northern area possessed a wild romantic beauty, having many small lochs and steep-sided glens through which burns rushed down to the sea. It was in great contrast to the serene farm fields of the east and the gentle slopes of the barren green hills of the west and the south.

It was not until the day before Tearlach was due to return to Torvaig that Penelope went to Cladach Bay. She came to it on a dull day on which rain threatened from blowsy grey clouds which chased one another across the perpetual movement of the pewter-coloured sea.

A perfect sickle of pale yellow sand edged the grey water. Several small cottages were scattered on the land behind the shore and behind them, set on the bare hillside, there was a small graveyard surrounded by a drystone wall.

Each cottage was separated from the next by fields in which the usual crops of barley, oats and rye were growing. As Penelope drove slowly down the road she noticed a young woman taking in washing from a line strung between a cottage wall and a byre. She stopped the car, helped the children out and went across the road to speak to the woman. As she had hoped, the woman was Molly Lang. She was about the same age as herself, had orangey-red hair, wide sea-green eyes and a friendly grin.

When she introduced herself, Molly nodded and said, 'Aye, Donald told me all about ye. Would ye like to be coming in for a cuppa?' She spoke in a thick Scottish brogue which did not have its origin in the Highlands. 'Bring the bairns in, too. I've a wee lass myself, but she's asleep just now. Do ye mind if I call ye Penny? I find Penelope a bit of a mouthful.'

Drinking tea in the homely, rumpled living room of the four-room cottage, while Isa and Davy played with wee Sheila's toys, Penelope learned that Molly and her husband had been eighteen months on the croft and liked it fine.

'We were both working in Glasgow, but we were tired of the city. Then Donald,

112

whose people came from Torvaig, saw the croft which had once belonged to his family being advertised. He wrote after it, had an interview with Mr. Gunn, who was wanting to attract people back to the island, and we came here to live. I look after the animals and help in the fields at harvest time and in the spring, and Don has plenty of mechanical work to do because he's the only mechanic living on the island just now. Ach, there's no life like it and wee Sheila is growing up healthy and bonny. Do ye think ye're going to like working at the big house?'

'I'm on probation for a month. You see, Mr. Gunn wanted someone older and wasn't pleased when he saw me,' replied Penelope.

'Aye, I can imagine ye were a bit of a surprise to him,' said Molly with a grin.

'Anyway, he says that if I'm not satisfactory I'll have to go at the end of four weeks.'

'Ach, he says that to everyone. It's his way to keep people on the hop, so that they'll do their best. He said the same to us. Gave us twelve months to show willing. He said the same to his own cousin Hugh. If at the end of twelve months Hugh hasn't worked his croft properly and hasn't made any income from his fishing and his painting, he'll have to go too.'

'Mr. Gunn is a hard man.'

'So he is, but he's fair too. I'd rather have him than one of those soft-spoken types who say one thing and do another. Ye know where ye are with him,' said Molly, pouring more tea. 'Have ye met Hugh?'

'Yes, I have, and his sister,' replied Penelope. 'I was thinking I'd call in to see them while I'm over this way. Which croft is his?'

'He lives at the other side of the bay where the road ends. He's a blithe laddie, and we've had some great evenings with him. Ye should hear him sing and play the guitar. But yon Kathleen is a different matter. I suppose it takes all sorts to make a world, but between you and me, she fancies herself a wee bit above the rest of us. She has her eye on Mr. Gunn, ye ken.'

'I had noticed. Does he have his eye on her?'

'I dinna ken, but I'm thinking he'd be a hard nut for any woman to crack.'

★　　　★　　　★

114

Later Penelope drove round the bay to the other side and called at Hugh's cottage. There was no answer to her knock. Glancing about her, she noticed a narrow road winding up the hillside to the graveyard and remembered what Hugh had said about the possibility that members of the Sandison family might have been buried there, so she decided to leave the car by Hugh's cottage and walk up the lane.

On the way she passed another house. Its walls, which had been newly painted white, gleamed in the pale sunlight which had just broken through the clouds. In the garden she could see heaps of earth beside a shallow trench and she realised that it must be Ian McTaggart's house. Driven by a sudden impulse, she went up to the plain black front door and knocked.

Ian McTaggart's clear grey eyes widened with surprise when he opened the door and saw Penelope and the children standing there.

'We came to visit Hugh, but he isn't in,' she explained. 'He told me that his sister is in partnership with you, so I thought she might be working here and would tell us where Hugh is.'

'Hugh is away to sea collecting his

lobster pots,' replied Ian in his slow sing-song voice. 'Kathleen is away also, with Tearlach to Edinburgh. She's been gone this past week.'

And I had thought he had merely been giving her a lift the day I saw her get into his car at the ferry, thought Penelope.

Aloud she said: 'Oh,' feeling slightly nonplussed, not wanting to leave, yet not sure how to stay. Ian seemed to sense her hesitancy, for he smiled and explained a little further.

'Kathleen and I are looking for new markets for our jewellery, and Tearlach, with his usual generosity, said he'd introduce us to people he knows who might be interested. Kathleen is much better at public relations than I am, so she went with him to meet them. Now that you're here, perhaps you'd like to come and see some of our work.'

'Yes. I'd like very much to see how you make your jewellery. I've often admired Scottish jewellery and I've a cairngorm brooch which used to be my grandmother's.'

In the house they were greeted excitedly by a lovely red setter called Duff. The interior was quite different from Molly's homely place and Penelope thought she could see the imprint of Kathleen's sense of design. In the living room, which was two rooms made into one, beautiful antique oak furniture was shown off to good effect against pale blue walls. Hand-woven curtains hung at the windows. Above the fireplace in the long room, simple wooden shelves were decorated with antique pewter jugs and hand-thrown pieces of pottery.

Ian led them from the main part of the house into a wing which he had added to the original building. When she entered this big barn-like room it seemed to Penelope that she had walked into the workshop of a small light engineering firm because there were several work benches and numerous tools about. Ian was soon showing her examples of his fine workmanship, pendants, brooches and rings made not only from silver but also from gold and pewter.

'Most of my designs come from plant forms or natural objects which I find washed up on the shores,' he said in answer to a question. 'Don't be surprised if you see me roaming along the coast of the island looking for worm-eaten driftwood, seaweed or bits of cork. I also look at cross-sections of plants and leaf-cells through a microscope and try to reproduce the shapes in silver, and the colour of them in enamel work, which I enjoy doing too.'

He showed her some of the enamel pieces, explaining the various techniques he used. Limoges was the simplest, but least durable. In cloisonné the silver was built up into retaining walls to keep separate the colours of the enamel, whereas the pliqué à jour could be compared to stained glass, with the light showing through the enamel.

'I like to think I've inherited my talent directly from my Pictish forebears. They really knew how to deal with metal,' said Ian with his pleasant, diffident smile. 'There were many living here, who originally came from Ireland and were expert at this sort of thing, but then so were the Vikings, and much of the old jewellery which has been found buried in the ground is Pictish in inspiration but executed by Viking craftsmen, pointing to the fusion of two cultures. Kathleen scoffs at me for being so interested in the past, but I can't help myself.'

'Neither can I,' confided Penelope.

'Then perhaps you wouldn't mind telling

me about that strange experience you had on your way here. Were you able to see the other people who were on the ship with you? Could you describe any of them?'

'I'm not sure. When I told Hugh and Mr. Gunn about it Mr. Gunn made fun of me and asked me if Hugh had been in my . . . I don't know what to call it?'

'Why not call it a dream? It was obviously your subconscious trying to tell you something,' suggested Ian gently. 'What was your answer to his question?'

'I tried to think back to it, as you do try to remember dreams, and I could only remember one of the men. He was like Mr. Gunn. So I decided that was because I'd been watching him just before I had the dream.'

'It could mean, you know, that when you came to Torvaig in a previous life, you were with him. Have you ever been *here* before?' asked Ian seriously.

She stared at him in bewilderment. His bearded face was familiar, but she could not be sure whether it was because she had become accustomed to seeing him that afternoon or because she had sat like this with him in another lifetime.

But then, she remembered, he had worn

119

the long habit of a monk and had sandals on his feet. She had seen him through the window of a small cell into which the sunlight had slanted, lending a glow to the pinkish stone from which it had been built.

Penelope blinked rapidly. How could she remember such an incident when as far as she knew it had never happened to her?

'I haven't been to Torvaig, but my grandmother was born here,' she said quickly.

'Maybe that is the explanation,' said Ian. 'Was her family here a long time?'

'I don't know. Mr. Guthrie says that the Sandison family held crofts for generations in Cladach, and Hugh has suggested that I should look in the old graveyard for a headstone which would show where the family grave is.'

'Let's go there now,' said Ian. 'Your young charges are getting a little restless and they might enjoy a walk with Duff, my dog.'

The red setter shook its tasselled tail with joy in anticipation of the walk with young companions, and they all set off up the lane as the pale sun slid from under a cloud again and bathed the hillside with yellow light.

The graveyard followed the slope of the land and was overgrown with tall grasses and bracken. A clump of rowan trees crowded in one corner beside the gate, planted there to keep the witches away. On the other side was a small broken-down chapel over whose walls wild roses twined. They peered in at the narrow window and Penelope recognised, with a shock, the cell in which she had just seen in her 'dream'.

She glanced quickly at Ian to see if he had recognised it too, and she noticed for the first time the fine bones of nose and jaw, the creamy pallor of the skin, the dreaminess of his grey eyes. Truly it was the face of an ascetic.

He became aware of her stare and turned to look at her.

'Well? Do you recognise the place?' he asked.

'Yes. Do you?'

'I've visited it before, but not until now have I felt so strongly that I might have known it in another lifetime. I feel today that once, a long time ago, I lived here in Achmore.'

'Did you say Achmore?' asked Penelope excitedly.

'I did. This group of crofts, I've

discovered recently, once had the name Achmore to distinguish it from the group nearer the shore, known as Cladach, which is the Gaelic name for shore.'

'Then that proves it,' said Penelope with a smile of satisfaction. 'My grandmother wasn't romancing. She did come from Torvaig and she lived in a place called Achmore. I can hardly wait to tell Mr. Gunn.'

At that point Isa, who had wandered off, fell amongst some brambles and rose briars. She let out a shrill shriek and had to be rescued by Ian.

'It will take time to clear this place,' he said when he returned to Penelope's side. 'It's impossible to search for a headstone while everything is overgrown. Shall we come back another day?'

Penelope agreed and they began to walk down the lane.

'Why is it necessary to prove to Tearlach that your grandmother wasn't romancing?' asked Ian.

'He refused to believe anything I told him about her,' she said, with more vehemence than she realised, and Ian gave her an amused sidelong glance, noting the pink flush on her cheeks and the sparkle in her mist-blue eyes.

'And he infuriated you,' he commented. 'He has a knack of doing that. I get the impression that you don't like him very much.'

'Let's say I have difficulty in understanding him,' said Penelope carefully. After all, she did not know Ian very well and he might relay anything she said about her employer to Kathleen, who might relay it in her turn to Tearlach.

'Do nannies take a course in diplomacy these days?' asked Ian teasingly. 'You can be frank with me, Penelope. I shan't betray you to anyone.'

Flushing slightly at this gently-phrased rebuke, she tried to put her feelings regarding her employer into words.

'I know he has done a great deal for the Torvaig and to help other people. Davy and Isa lack nothing in the way of material goods, but I can't help feeling he's cold and hard, almost heartless. He doesn't seem to love them.'

'Or anyone else, for that matter, or so it seems,' added Ian soberly, nodding his head. 'I know what you mean. There's an inner wall which he has built up over the years to prevent anyone from knowing his real feelings. Behind that wall none of us are allowed to penetrate. Yet on the surface he's friendly, outgoing. I have my own theory about that inner wall.'

'What is that?'

'It's based on what Kathleen has told me about Tearlach. His mother died when he was only eight, soon after his sister was born. His father married again, more for convenience than anything else, and from the first Tearlach loathed his stepmother. It was she who drove him to the desperate action of running away from home before he had finished school.'

'He doesn't seem to have had any affection for his sister, either,' said Penelope, and told him what Tearlach had said about Avis when she had offered him sympathy.

'Yet she asked him to take care of her children. She knew, of course, that they would benefit,' mused Ian.

'They are benefiting, materialistically speaking.'

'But not in the way you think they should. Yet why should you worry about them?' asked Ian.

'I'm just made that way, I suppose. I can't bear to see children rejected.'

'Then you'd have felt sorry for Tearlach when he was a boy, ignored by his father, rejected by his stepmother and with no one to turn to. Maybe that's why he finds it difficult to love or show love in the way you mean. He's very lucky at cards, you know, and it doesn't do to play with him for money, for he invariably wins, as Hugh and I know to our cost,' Ian replied with a laugh.

'I see. He's lucky at cards but unlucky in love.'

'It seems to be that way. Do you know, Penelope, I've a curious feeling that you and I have discussed someone in this way before?'

'I've the same feeling,' she said seriously. 'Only then you were wearing a monk's habit.'

'Are you sure?' he exclaimed.

'Quite sure.'

'This is very exciting. My name, McTaggart, means "son of a priest", and I have a theory that there were some Pictish priests already living on Torvaig when the Vikings came,' he said in awed tones. 'They were hermits and had their settlement here at Achmore. I base my theory on the artefacts which Hugh and I have found when we've been excavating.'

'Have you found more tools?'

'Yes, made of slate and stone, such as the Picts used. We've also found the remains of a building, but its masonry technique is like that used by the Picts in Ireland, and I think that possibly the Vikings used the dispossessed Picts as their slaves to build their dwellings.'

'But couldn't Magnus Gunn have brought them from Ireland as he brought his wife?'

'That's possible too.' Ian glanced thoughtfully towards the bay. 'There's Hugh coming back,' he said, pointing to an open fishing boat which was chugging into the bay. 'Let's go down and tell him about your most recent flashback. I know he's interested in your experience too.'

Ian's excitement was infectious and by the time they had reached the jetty as Hugh brought his fishing boat alongside, Penelope felt just as excited. It was like getting high on history, she thought, and wondered when her next flashback would take place.

Hugh stepped ashore, seeming bigger than ever in his glistening oilskins. Beyond him in the boat Penelope could see the openwork lobster pots in which the mottled blue lobsters were moving.

'How did you get here?' he greeted her. Briefly she explained about the car and he whistled. 'Makes me think that perhaps someone is doing his best to encourage you to stay rather than drive you away. Are you still on probation?'

'Yes, I'm afraid so. He hasn't been here all week, so I haven't had a chance to blot my copy book again, although I did blot it rather badly, more than once, before he left.'

'Why? What did you do?' asked Hugh, his eyes gleaming inquisitively.

'I just told him what I felt about his attitude to the children and how material goods, like toys and games, can never take the place of real love and attention.'

Again Hugh whistled, and then with a touch of mockery murmured, 'What are you trying to do, Penelope? Are you hoping to make the old lion change his ways by behaving like Mary Poppins? Better take care. You can be sure he's adding up those blots, and when the end of your probationary period comes he'll be balancing them against your credit side and deducting them. He's doing the same with me. That's why I haven't been over to see you.'

'I wondered why.'

'I was warned off,' said Hugh, with a slightly sheepish grin.

'By Mr. Gunn?' Penelope's eyes were wide.

'Yes. You see, Miss Jones, you and I are here to work and we needn't think we can play together during working hours. Get the message?'

'Yes. I had an impression he was suspicious of us on the yacht,' murmured Penelope, seething inwardly at Tearlach Gunn's assumption that she was involved with Hugh.

Davy was showing an interest in the lobsters and Hugh squatted down beside him to tell him about them.

'Isn't this one a beauty?' he said, and glancing up at Penelope, he added, 'Stay and have tea with Ian and me. I can offer you lobster thermidor à la Drummond.'

'I'd love to, but I think I'd better go back. The children are tired.'

'Then come back later this evening, when they've gone to bed,' suggested Ian.

Regretfully thinking how much she would have enjoyed spending the evening with this quiet, shy and yet interesting man, Penelope declined again.

'I'm sorry, but I have to stay with them. Davy sometimes wakes up and someone has to be there,' she explained.

'Surely Tearlach isn't slave-driving,' Ian murmured, and she glanced at him sharply. Once more he was the hermit priest of her earlier vision and she was the slave girl brought to Torvaig by the first Magnus Gunn so long ago. 'Don't you have any free time?' he added.

'I forgot to ask him before he left. If I do have time off, it means someone else will have to look after Davy and Isa, and I can't imagine Mr. Gunn doing that,' she replied.

'When is he coming back?' asked Hugh.

'Tomorrow.'

'Then I suggest that the mice should play while the big cat is away. Ian and I will come and see you since you can't come and see us. Will eight o'clock this evening be suitable?'

Penelope agreed, pleased at the thought of having visitors, and drove back to Torvaig House happily having enjoyed her afternoon. She felt quite at home on the hillside at Achmore, which was to be expected since her grandmother's ancestors had lived there for such a long time. She and Ian McTaggart had known each other very well in that other life, she thought, when he had been a priest and she had been in thrall to a Viking.

She shook her head vigorously. She must stop having these strange feelings. She remembered her grandmother talking about Gaelic women who had possessed the second sight and had been able to foretell the future, but she had never heard of anyone whose visions had been of the past! If she wasn't careful she would be living her life as the unnamed slave girl whose colouring had been like her own, and that would never do!

After she had put the children to bed that evening she went down to the kitchen to tell Mrs. Guthrie that Ian and Hugh were coming over later. She found the housekeeper busy baking in preparation for the invasion of guests the next day.

'Then we'll have a wee *ceilidh* in our sitting room down here,' said Mrs. Guthrie. 'Ach, I love to hear Hugh playing his guitar and singing those saucy Scottish songs he picked up when he was a student.'

'There's something else I want to ask you,' said Penelope, a little diffidently.

'Ask away, lass,' replied the kindly woman as she rolled pastry with a few deft strokes of her rolling pin.

'It's a ticklish subject. Did Mr. Gunn say anything to you about me having any time off?'

'I suppose you'd like to be going somewhere with Hugh?' said Mrs. Guthrie with a knowing twinkle in her eyes. 'Well, that's natural enough with you both being about the same age. And I'm thinking you should be entitled to a few hours off. I'd be more than willing to keep an eye on the bairns for you.'

Penelope shook her head negatively.

'Oh, no. I don't want to do anything unless it has Mr. Gunn's approval, and I just wondered if he'd said anything to you about my free time.'

'No, but then I didn't expect him to. I suppose he went away in such a hurry he forgot to mention it to you. You can ask him about it tomorrow when he comes home,' said Mrs. Guthrie practically.

Penelope looked down at her hands and then up again, a faintly rueful grin curving her lips.

'I was hoping to avoid having to do that and that's why I'm asking you. You see, every time Mr. Gunn and I meet we seem to strike sparks off each other, and since I'm only here on probation for a month I'd like to avoid the risk of annoying him and so losing my job,' she explained.

Mrs. Guthrie cocked a shrewd eye in Penelope's direction. 'Striking sparks, eh? And how would you be doing that?' she asked.

'I don't know. It just happens. He says something and I over-react, and before I know what I've done I've said things I shouldn't say to an employer,' explained Penelope.

'Humph. Well, that's something only you can sort out for yourself, lass. But if it's any help I don't mind asking him about you having free time because it stands to reason you should have it. I'm only surprised he didn't say anything to you before he went away. He's usually very particular about such things.'

Grateful for and relieved by Mrs. Guthrie's offer to ask Tearlach Gunn about her time off, Penelope was able to relax and enjoy the visit of Ian and Hugh. The Guthries made the two young men welcome as only Highlanders can, and when their eldest son and his wife arrived bringing with them another young couple, who lived on the island, the wee *ceilidh* which Mrs. Guthrie had promised turned out to be a much larger one with Hugh playing his guitar and Aileen Guthrie singing, and Alec Guthrie, after much persuasion from the others, bringing out his bagpipes and playing a *pibroch*, which is a series of variations composed especially for the bagpipes.

Thinking she had seldom enjoyed an evening so much, Penelope went to bed happily and lay thinking for a while about Ian and Hugh. For the first time in her life she knew what it was to be friendly with two young men on an equal footing. Neither of them expected anything from her other than her friendship, she was sure. The only other man she had ever known well was Brian, and he had expected too much! When she had said good night to them, they had made her promise to go over the Cladach as soon as she had some free time, and together they would take her to the old graveyard to search for a headstone bearing the name Sandison.

If she hadn't come to Torvaig she would never have known what it was like to have such friends, she thought sleepily, and she must not let anyone drive her away from her home, now that she had found it.

★　　　★　　　★

Next day, in the late afternoon, Tearlach arrived back at Torvaig House, closely followed by two other cars which brought his guests. Penelope did not see them arrive, but knew they had come because Mrs. Guthrie came upstairs to tell her, and to say that Miss Drummond was also in the house acting as hostess for the laird.

Both children were in bed and Penelope was about to sit down at the small writing desk in her room to write to an old school friend who was also a nanny, when a wail from Davy's room sent her scurrying in there. He started to complain that his uncle hadn't come to see him and with a sigh Penelope began the usual efforts to distract him. She was just coming to the end of a story when the door opened and Tearlach came in. Davy greeted him with a shriek of delight and flung himself out of bed to clutch him round the legs. Coolly disengaging himself from this ecstatic embrace, Tearlach bade him sternly to get back into bed and told Penelope to finish reading the story.

Rather embarrassed by his presence while she was reading, she finished the story in a monotonous voice, most unlike the usual dramatic one which she usually used when reading to Davy and was aware that her employer, who was standing by the window looking out, was listening to every word. When she had finished, she closed the book, kissed Davy on the cheek as he snuggled down in bed, and then went through the communicating door into her room, closing the door behind her.

She had only been in the room a few seconds when the door was wrenched open again and Tearlach stepped through it, closing it rather violently behind him.

'I came to talk to you, not to get involved in a good-night session with my nephew,' he grated. 'What's all this about you wanting time off?'

Sometimes the roughness shows, Hugh had said, and this was one of the times. Obviously Mrs. Guthrie had lost no time in informing him of the nanny's request for time off, and the effect seemed to be disastrous, thought Penelope ruefully as she noted the unpleasant twist to his mouth and the anger flickering in his narrowed

135

eyes.

She swallowed hard, rubbed the palms of her hands against her skirt, a sure sign she was nervous, and squared up to him.

'I asked Mrs. Guthrie if any arrangements had been made for me to have time off and she said she'd ask you about it,' she said.

'Why couldn't you ask me yourself?' he rapped back at her.

'You weren't here,' she replied sweetly, and to her alarm he swore at her and interrupted her rudely.

'Don't come the innocent with me! I know I haven't been here. What I meant was you should have asked me when I was here, or now that I've come back.'

She wondered if he had guessed she had wanted to avoid another run-in with him and was annoyed with her about that, for some reason, but she had no answer to his question other than the one that she had wanted to avoid him, so she said nothing.

Her silence seemed to irritate him even more. Advancing towards her he stood with his hands on his hips and glared down at her.

'Come on, out with it. Why couldn't you ask me yourself?'

'Shush!' she murmured, putting a finger to her lips. 'You'll wake Isa.'

His straight white teeth snapped together audibly as he gritted them and refrained from swearing at her again.

'Since you won't answer my question I'll answer it for you. You didn't ask me for time off yourself because you were afraid you'd lose your temper again and say what you feel, and that might lead you to being sacked before the end of the month. Isn't that so?'

She nodded dumbly. The anger seeped out of his face leaving it strangely tired-looking. He swung away from her and went over to the window. When he spoke again his usually vibrant voice was flat and dreary.

'I'd thought better of *you*,' he muttered obscurely, and there was a little silence, while Penelope wondered what to say, as she stood in the middle of the room looking at his broad hunched shoulders and shaggy mane of hair.

'Anyone on this island will tell you I've no time for the oblique approach,' he went on slowly. 'I'm your employer, not Mrs. Guthrie. If you want to know anything about the children or about the conditions

137

of your employment here, you come straight to me. You don't go behind my back. Is that clear?' He turned to look at her.

'Yes, Mr. Gunn,' she said with a touch of breathlessness as understanding dawned. He preferred it when she bearded him in his den. She should have rememberd he had said to her at their first meeting that she should never apologise for saying what she felt to him. 'Please could you tell me how much free time I'm allowed in this job?' she added hurriedly.

His glance was enigmatic.

'That's better,' he murmured. 'How much time off did you get in your last job? I hope you're not going to tell me that there's a nannies' union and that I've been breaking their regulations.'

'No, as far as I know, there isn't,' replied Penelope seriously. 'In my last job I had two half days each week and a full weekend every month, but that was a different situation from the one here because the children were with their parents when I was off.'

He nodded his understanding and turned to look out of the window again as if giving her statement some thought.

'If I allow you time off what will you do with it? Where will you go?' he asked.

'I shall attend to personal necessities such as shopping and mending, and I shall explore the island, although I don't really think I have to account to you for those hours of freedom, even if you are my employer,' she replied crisply.

His head turned sharply at that and he gave her one of those unnerving narrow-eyed stares.

'That's true, you don't. I'm just trying to make sure that you don't intend to make mischief at my expense as the last nanny did,' he said coldly. 'Then you shall have, for the time being, a half day and one whole day off every alternate week, starting with a half day this coming Wednesday. The following week it will be all of Saturday. Whether you will ever get any more free time is entirely up to you, as it's just possible you'll be packing your bags when your four-week probation period is up and leaving Torvaig for good. Will that suit you?'

'Yes, thank you. And I shan't be leaving Torvaig, Mr. Gunn.'

He came across and stood in front of her and grinned down at her. The tired look had gone and the vibrancy was back in his voice.

'I wouldn't be too sure about that, Miss Jones,' he said softly. 'Did you invite Hugh and Ian here last night or did they invite themselves?'

'Hugh invited himself and Ian. I met them yesterday when I was over at Achmore,' she replied, wondering a little uneasily what lay behind his question and deciding that since he didn't like what he called an 'oblique' approach she had better be scrupulously honest with him at all times.

'When you were where?' he demanded, making no effort to hide his surprise.

'Achmore.' She couldn't help sounding smug. 'That's the name of the group of crofts up on the hill at Cladach Bay. You told me there was no place with that name on Torvaig.'

'Because I didn't know. This is the first I've heard of it. Why did you go there?'

'I wanted to see the graveyard which Hugh had told me about. I called on Molly Lang and then went on to find Hugh. He was fishing, so I walked up to the graveyard and called on Mr. McTaggart thinking I might find Miss Drummond there. But she was away too, with you in Edinburgh.' His quick frown came. Obviously he did not like her reference to Kathleen. 'Mr. McTaggart went with me to the graveyard and it was there that he told me the name of the group of crofts. And it may interest you to know that Mr. Guthrie has already told me that my grandmother's father, Hector Sandison, left Torvaig and went to live in England because the old laird wouldn't make improvements on the island.'

He stared at her for a moment and then burst out laughing.

'How you enjoyed telling me all that!' he remarked. 'Very well, I'll concede that round to you. I really don't know much about Torvaig's past or about the people who used to live here. All I'm interested in is its present and future, and the people who live here now. There's been too much looking over the shoulder at the past in this part of the country and it hasn't done anyone any good at all.'

'Do you accept, then, that my reason for coming here was to see where my grandmother was born?' persisted Penelope.

'I do now. When you told me on the boat coming here it seemed a little far-fetched

141

and I admit to being suspicious of you. Even so I'm sure it wasn't your only reason. You're on the run from something. What happened? What did he do to you? Did he find another woman?'

Her resolve not to let him rouse her anger was almost destroyed by his abrupt, rather crude way of describing Brian's behaviour. She went pink with pain. He had no right to probe so carelessly in a wound which she had hoped was well on the way to being healed.

'Supposing he did, what has it to do with you?' she hissed.

'Nothing really. I'm just curious to find out if my hunch about you is correct. You've a bruised look about you that young woman sometimes get when they think they've been defeated in the game they call love,' he replied, his shrewd gaze never leaving her face.

'How can you possibly tell? What do you know about love?' she flung at him wildly, hoping to make a hit somewhere

'Again, nothing.' he said. 'At least I know nothing about that romantic mushy feeling which women often confuse with love, which puts a man on a pedestal and dehumanises him. I deal in realities, not in romances.'

'Oh yes, anyone can see that,' she flared. 'You heap material goods on two little children, thinking that gifts will make up for your lack of real affection for them.'

'Are we back in that groove again?' he mocked. 'You're getting monotonous, Miss Jones.'

'I daresay you've done the same to women in your time,' she rushed on, heedless now of the danger in saying too much. 'Buying them with gifts, but making sure they get nothing of you.'

'And to think you once accused me of being prejudiced!' he jibed.

Why didn't he go? thought Penelope wildly. Why was he here in her room tormenting her, trying to make her lose her temper and tell him home truths about himself so that he could accuse her of rudeness and sack her? Why didn't he go back downstairs to his guests and to Kathleen Drummond?

She raised her head and said in a voice which quivered, 'This is my room, Mr. Gunn, given to me for my private use. Would you mind leaving? I have a letter to write before I go to bed.'

'To your grandmother, to tell her you've

found the place where she was born?' he taunted, not moving an inch.

'My grandmother died two years ago,' she said patiently, although her heart was beating so hard she thought it would burst.

'To your parents, then?' he persisted.

'My parents died when I was very young.'

'No grandmother, no parents. So you're all alone in the world, and lonely, pining for the man who got away,' he jeered. 'You're breaking my heart, Miss Jones,' he added sarcastically.

For the first time in her life Penelope literally saw red. Of its own will, or so it seemed, her right hand swung up, aiming for the handsome sun-tanned face inches above her own. It was half-way there when her common sense asserted itself. If she hit him he would have good cause to dismiss her, and judging by the expectant mocking gleam in his eyes he was waiting for her to make a wrong move, maddening man that he was.

With a great effort she forced her arm to change direction and crossing it with her left arm, she took a deep steadying breath and said, as coolly as she could:

'But that's impossible, Mr. Gunn. You

haven't a heart to break.'

He smiled, and she was watching him so closely that she was able to see that his smile began in his eyes as a distinct twinkle before it spread to his mouth. A person who could smile like that must have a heart, she thought contrarily.

'That was a very close thing,' he murmured, and then glanced at his watch. 'But I've no more time for brawling, much as I enjoy it. About your time off, make it every Wednesday afternoon until midnight instead of every other Wednesday and every alternate Saturday from nine in the morning until midnight, and be sure to be back by midnight or you'll be in trouble. Don't get lost when you're exploring, and beware getting too entangled with red-haired Viking types or you might get hurt again. Good night, Nanny.'

With another tantalising grin he turned and went from the room. Penelope let out a long shuddering breath, flopped down on the divan and pounded one of the cushions with her fists.

Hateful, tormenting man, pricking and prodding at her, rousing a temper she had not known she possessed until she met him, then retreating behind a charming, yet

145

strangely indulgent smile. How dared he warn her against Hugh, and then call her Nanny! Oh, how she wished she could have slapped him! There was certainly no danger of her ever putting *him* on a pedestal!

She punched the cushion with all the force she could muster, then to her surprise, she burst into tears and cried, something she had not done for years, not even when she had learned about Brian's deception of her. After a while she sat up, blew her nose and wiped her eyes. She felt much better, as if the storm of tears had released an inner tension.

For a while she sat in the gloaming, considering her violent reaction to her employer's remarks. Was it possible that with his own brand of mockery he had cauterised the wound inflicted on her sensibility by Brian's treatment of her, and which had been festering? Perhaps now she would really begin to forget that for two whole years she had been taken in by a handsome philanderer, who had duped her into believing he was in love with her. One thing was sure, she would never allow herself to be duped again. Mr. Gunn need have no fear, she would never become too entangled with his cousin Hugh, or with any other man, if she could help it. From now on all her friendships with the opposite sex were going to be completely harmless to herself.

During the next few days squally weather hit the island, but the wind and rain did not prevent the guests from going out of doors. Every day Penelope saw them leaving the house on their way to fish the island's numerous lochs and burns. Usually, but not always, they were accompanied by Tearlach, and sometimes by Kathleen.

From Mrs. Guthrie, Penelope learned that the guests were two married couples and that they were interested in the jewellery which Ian and Kathleen were making.

'That's why Miss Drummond has been over here, helping to entertain them, acting as hostess, you might say. Ach, the house needs a mistress, so it does, and I wouldn't be surprised if they didn't make a match of it one of these days,' said the plump jolly housekeeper one day, when Penelope had joined her and her husband for elevenses in the kitchen. She loved to romance about Tearlach and was always looking forward to the day when he would settle down and marry.

'But I thought Miss Drummond and Mr. Gunn were cousins, and that he was a confirmed bachelor,' said Penelope, who loved to tease Mrs. Guthrie, in the kindest, gentlest way.

'So was I until I met Bessie,' put in Alec Guthrie, following her lead. 'But I was no proof against a determined woman and look at me now, thirty-five years married.'

'Any regrets?' asked Penelope.

'Not I. Ach, we've had our disagreements, but we've always been able to compromise. We've always needed each other.'

'Then you've been very fortunate,' said Penelope. 'What makes you think Miss Drummond will be able to change Mr. Gunn's attitude, Mrs. Guthrie?'

'Well, it stands to reason a man in his position should have a wife, now he has a home. It was different when he was knocking about the world. And they're not close cousins and they get on very well together. Then you can't deny she's a beautiful woman. If he'd been married he wouldn't have had to ask Alec and me to come and live in when you came to work here, and he wouldn't have to invite a

148

single woman to act as hostess to his guests,' replied Mrs. Guthrie.

'Maybe he prefers it that way,' said Alec musingly. 'If Miss Drummond or Miss Jones do anything to displease him he can tell them to leave. It's not so easy to get rid of a wife. And then it's not every young woman that wants to get married these days. They're an independent lot, if what I read in the newspapers is true.'

'Aye, I've read all that nonsense about women wanting to have the same freedom as men,' growled Mrs. Guthrie. 'A lot of rubbish, I call it. Any woman who believes that marriage makes a slave of her, or a second class citizen, needs her head seeing to. Marriage is the best career there is for a woman, and I haven't noticed our daughter thinking any differently from me. What about you, Penelope? Wouldn't you like to get married and have children?'

'Only if I could find someone who would respect me and treat me as an equal. As for children, I would just as soon look after other people's. There are so many children in the world who do not get the proper attention and treatment, even from their own parents, that I think there's a need for men and women, who don't have children, to help look after the rejected and the parentless.'

'Aye, I can see your point there, lass,' said Mrs. Guthrie accommodatingly, 'but I wouldn't mind betting that in a year or so you'll have found the man who respects you and treats you right and you'll be wanting to have his children. You won't be able to help yourself. And now, miss, I'm told you're to have this afternoon off and I'm to mind the bairns for you. So I'd be much obliged to you if you'd bring young Davy down here after lunch. He can help me with the baking. He likes nothing better than to cut pastry shapes and make gingerbread men.'

Having done her much-needed washing and mending, Penelope set off soon after two o'clock to walk over to Cladach Bay. She had learned from Alec Guthrie that it was possible to walk there by way of a path which ran across the headland which jutted out into the sea north of An Tigh Camus, which was the Gaelic name for the Bay of the House where Torvaig House was situated.

As she was leaving the house she noticed Tearlach Gunn's black car sweep up to the front door. It was driven by Donald Lang who sometimes acted as a chauffeur when he wasn't repairing machinery. Pausing on her way across the lawn, she turned back to see who had arrived and was not surprised to see Kathleen Drummond step out of the car. She was wearing blue jeans and white high-necked sweater and she was carrying a canvas zipped bag. As she went up the steps to the house the front door opened and Tearlach came out to greet her. He held out a hand to her which she took and when she reached his side, she reached up and kissed him on the cheek.

Penelope lingered only to see him guide his cousin into the house. It looked very much as if Mrs. Guthrie had been right in her prediction that the laird and his beautiful cousin might make a match of it, if indeed they hadn't already, she thought, as she followed the path which led from the sandy shore over the headland. She could imagine both of them ignoring the conventions and carrying on a fairly torrid affair without blessing it with the name of love or the dignity of marriage.

'Why so sour, Penelope?' she whispered to herself, as she scrambled up the rocky incline. 'Just because you didn't have the courage to throw convention to the winds

151

and indulge in that sort of relationship with Brian, why be critical of others? Anyway, it isn't any business of yours. You're here to do a job, to look after two motherless children, and you're jolly lucky to be able to do your job in such a lovely place, amongst such pleasant people as Bessie and Alec Guthrie, and all the others you've met since you came here.'

Having put herself in her place, she lifted her head to the sky and smelled the clear fresh air. Beneath her feet the grass was short and springy, starred with sea-thrift and small Scottish bluebells. The clouds of morning were lifting slowly as a faint breath of wind from the north blew them away. Blue sky appeared and pale sunlight glinted on the grey sea, changing its colour to gold-shot green. As she mounted to the top of the headland she could see the distant Outer Hebrides showing blue-black against a backcloth of eggshell green sky. Nearer, the dark points of the Shiant Isles loomed, spectacular cones of rock rearing up out of the sea.

Suddenly she felt again the feeling that she had been there before. She had stood on that spot and had looked out to sea. But then there had been longing in her heart as she had searched the wide expanse of water for the shape of a ship returning home to Torvaig; that same Viking ship in which she had come.

Shaking her head to clear it of the fantasy, she glanced down into An Tigh Camus, to the white two-masted boat which swung at its mooring. On the water to the right of it there was movement. The dinghy was speeding across the bay, its wake a white furrow of churned up water. It slowed down as it approached the yacht, and swung round to go alongside.

The sun, bursting forth in its full strength, glinted on the chromium-plated fittings of the yacht, as it swayed slightly as someone climbed aboard. It glinted also on Tearlach Gunn's blond-streaked hair and he turned to help someone else aboard. He was helping Kathleen, of course, and behind her came one of the guests. Then the dinghy, steered by Hugh, whose red-gold hair also caught the sun's light, was off, roaring back to the jetty to pick up the rest of the party.

Green serpents of envy coiled within Penelope's mind as she watched Kathleen step down into the cockpit and then disappear into the cabin. They were all going for a cruise and she longed to be going too. In fact she felt it was her right to be going, not Kathleen's.

Disconcerted by the strength of her jealousy and unable to account for it, she turned and ran until she could no longer see An Tigh Camus, and Cladach bay was in sight. Steadfastly keeping her thoughts away from the scene she had just witnessed, she scrambled down the rocky path which led to the shore and by the time she had reached the road which curved round the bay, envy was banished and she was in control of her feelings again.

Reaching the end of the lane which led to Achmore, she turned into it and went towards the house of Ian McTaggart.

CHAPTER FOUR

Penelope found Ian in his workshop. He was leaning over a delicately-twisted piece of silver which was clamped in a vice on the bench, and he was using a small coping saw to cut shapes in the fine metal. He showed he was aware of her presence by glancing at her and smiling, then turned to concentrate

154

on the intricate work he was doing.

Waiting for him to finish before she talked to him, she had time to study his face. His neatly-trimmed moustache and beard combined to draw attention to the sensitivity of his mouth. Above his wide-set grey eyes his fine dark eyebrows arched intelligently making three horizontal creases in his high forehead, which was partially hidden by his brushed-forward hair.

He was, she thought, a man of gentle disposition whose emotions were well disciplined. She could not imagine him hurting anyone, yet judging by his face she guessed he was very vulnerable to hurt inflicted on him by other people.

At last he laid the small saw aside, released the piece of silver from the vice and held it out to her.

'What is it?' she asked, turning it over between her fingers and marvelling at the workmanship. It was triangular in shape, a fine web of filigree silver.

'It's a pendant.'

'It makes me think of the skeleton of a leaf.'

'You're right,' he replied. 'It's intended to represent the shape of a birch leaf. Is this your day off?'

She looked up to answer the smile in his eyes with a smile of her own.

'It is. I'm free until midnight, and every other Saturday too. You look as if you're very busy.'

'I have been. The other day I was visited by the guests staying in the big house. One of them is a buyer from a big jewellery house in London, which has branches all over Britain. The other is a well-known Scottish business man. The buyer wanted to buy Kathleen's and my entire stock, the other ordered several pieces to be made for his wife and his daughter.'

In spite of the orders he had received he did not seem to be particularly happy, thought Penelope, noticing lines of strain around his eyes and mouth.

'Aren't you pleased?' she asked, handing the pendant back to him.

'Of course. An artist likes to have his work appreciated,' he replied rather drearily. 'I'm grateful to Tearlach. Without his interest this wouldn't have happened. He has contacts and influence.'

'Because he has money,' said Penelope shortly.

'Sometimes it can be a blessing, you

156

know,' Ian reproved her gently. 'People like myself and Hugh, and even you, would not be able to put our talents to good use if there were not people like Tearlach, who has the heart of a lion and is quite fearless when it comes to taking chances with money. With the support of the London jeweller he's willing to finance an exhibition of Kathleen's and my work in London in December.'

'I suppose you're right,' she admitted. 'He's taken them all sailing. I saw them going aboard as I came over the headland.'

'A cruise, I believe, to the Outer Hebrides, to the islands of Barra and Uist,' said Ian, a rather troubled frown darkening his face. 'Was Kathleen with them?'

'Yes, and Hugh. Didn't they tell you they were going?'

'I knew about Hugh, but Kathleen was not sure whether there would be room for her on the yawl.' His frown was deeper and his sensitive mouth looked taut as if he was having difficulty in hiding his feelings. 'She's been at the big house a lot recently!'

'Yes. She's been acting as hostess for Mr. Gunn. Mrs. Guthrie says she would be surprised if Mr. Gunn doesn't marry her,' replied Penelope, and watched the colour drain out of Ian's face.

'I suppose that's possible,' he said huskily. 'You're at the big house all the time. Have you noticed anything between them? No, don't bother to answer. I can see by your face that you have.'

He turned away ostensibly to tidy the tools on the bench, and Penelope stared at him, not knowing what to say as understanding dawned and she realised that he was in love with Kathleen. She wanted to question him about his feelings, but hesitated because she guessed, like most of his countrymen, he was reticent about discussing such matters. While she hesitated he turned back and making an effort to throw off his melancholy, smiled at her again, and said,

'I've done enough work for today and it's your day off. Outside the sun is shining at last. Shall we go and look at the headstones in the graveyard? Hugh and I have cleared away some of the undergrowth.'

'I was hoping you would come with me. That's why I called on you, and I must tell you that on my way here I had another of those strange flashbacks,' she said, touched by his interest and wishing to distract him from his obviously unhappy thoughts. 'Do

158

you think there's something wrong with me? Am I going out of my mind?'

He laughed a little and put an arm across her shoulders to guide her to the door.

'Not at all, Penelope. You strike me as being one of the sanest people I've ever met. No, I think that, like me, you're wholly Gael and as a result have one foot in the past and one foot in the present, and that coming back here, where your forebears lived for so long, has awakened your inherited memory. You're responding to the spirits of the people who once lived here. It isn't unusual for that to happen.'

'I hope you're right. But Mr. Gunn's forebears lived here too and he doesn't have any flashbacks. In fact he told me he had no time for the past of Torvaig, that it was only its present and future that interest him.'

'But then Tearlach, for all his name, is no Gael really. He was brought up in the city of Glasgow and his mother was English. It seems as if he has inherited her practical realistic attitude to life, which is just as well for Torvaig, when you come to think about it seriously. Torvaig needed Tearlach as much as he needed Torvaig.'

'What do you mean by that?'

159

'I have the impression he was tired of wandering and that he wanted a home. Torvaig provides both that and a challenge as well, something which is very necessary to a man of his temperament.'

It was strange, thought Penelope, how often they talked about the laird. It wasn't only she who found him a powerful and dominating personality, but as none of them would have been there on Torvaig if he had not returned to the island, it was only natural that he should loom large in their conversation.

She had never thought of a graveyard as being a pleasant place in which to spend a sunny afternoon, but the one at Achmore was so pretty with its rose-entwined chapel, peaceful and scented in the warm mild air, that she forgot Ian's unhappiness and her own dark primitive feelings when she had watched Kathleen going aboard Tearlach's yacht. Wandering around with Ian she felt closer than ever to the past life of the island, as she peered at the names and dates on the headstones, some of which were so old and moss-covered, that it was difficult to make out the carved letters.

At last they found one bearing the name Sandison. On it were listed several Hectors and their wives and other members of their families. The last date was mid-nineteenth century and Penelope assumed that the Hector who had been buried then had been the father of her grandmother's father.

'I wish that Grandmother could have come here just once before she died,' she whispered, looking down the hill at the sea. Far away sunlight glinted briefly on white sails. Then the gleam was lost and she wondered if she had imagined that there was a sailing boat out there on the wide expanse of glittering water.

'Wasn't it possible for her to come?' asked Ian.

'I think when she was young she didn't think about it, being too busy bringing up my father and his two sisters. Then later, after my parents were both killed in a train crash, she was too busy going to work to keep me.'

His glance was keen as he watched her watching the distant smudge on the water, which was the big yacht and which he had also seen.

'Like the laird, you're one of the lonely ones,' he murmured, and took one of her hands in his.

Surprised by his words as well as by his

warm sympathetic gesture, she could not help comparing him to the absent Tearlach. He offered gentleness instead of jibing sarcasm, soothing her instead of rousing her.

'Come and have tea with me,' he said, 'and then afterwards we'll talk about Torvaig's past and I'll show you the excavation and the few artefacts Hugh and I have uncovered.'

And so the rest of the afternoon and the evening passed in a pleasant blur, and when the long Hebridean twilight touched hill and sea with mysterious shadows, Ian walked back with her over the headland and along the shore. He left her where the lawn swept down from the house to touch the pale sand, and she stood for a while watching him return along the shore, stopping now and again to pick up a shell or some other piece of flotsam which had caught his observant artist's eye.

'Come to Achmore again, on your day off,' he had invited, when he had left her, and she knew she would go, not only because she was attracted by the quiet sensitive man but also because she felt she could ease in some way the heartache from which she guessed he was suffering.

She turned to go across the lawn to the house and immediately her tranquil mood was shattered, as smooth glass is shattered by a stone. In turning her glance was caught by the red mooring buoy bobbing on the water. Devoid of colour in the twilight, it looked dark and lonely, giving the bay a desolate appearance because the big yawl had gone, and she was shaken suddenly by a feeling of forlornness as if someone she loved dearly had gone from her.

Frightened by the feeling, she whirled and turning her back on the empty bay, she hurried up to the house, which, pale and ghostly, was silent and without light amongst the dark still trees. Here too was an atmosphere of desolation, of emptiness, as if the owner had left the house and would never return.

Her heart thumping madly, Penelope walked quickly round the side of the house and saw, to her relief, a light shining out from the Guthries' sitting room. Quietly she let herself in through the side door and went upstairs to her room.

The yawl was gone from the bay for ten days. Each time Penelope looked out at the bobbing red buoy, alone on the shimmering water, she experienced that strange aching feeling, as if she had been bereft, and she would look away quickly.

Most of the time, however, she was too busy to question the feeling and wonder whether it was her own or an inherited one. The spell of fine weather made getting about easy and she and the children visited most of the island's little coves and beaches in turn. Once, much to Davy's delight, they went to the mainland on the ferry.

Wednesday came round again and she used her time off to call on Molly Lang. Then she walked up to the old graveyard. As a matter of course, she called on Ian to find him still working on the jewellery he had promised to have ready for Tearlach's guests, when they returned from their cruise. Once more Penelope stayed for tea, but when she walked back to Torvaig House she was by herself enjoying the golden afterglow of the sunset.

She was beginning to feel very much at home and was surprised to find that only three and a half weeks had passed since she had first set foot on the island. Next Monday her four weeks' probation would be ended, and she knew that she was coping satisfactorily with the children.

Although Davy still showed signs of having a nervous temperament, she was becoming more and more convinced that he had inherited it from his Spanish father, and that it was nothing to do with him having lost both parents. He was naturally volatile, swinging from fierce passionate tempers to happy gaiety. He did not like the rain or the wind and would obstinately refuse to go out on such days, but when the sun shone he responded to its warmth like a flower.

On the other hand, Isa was a placid, complacent child, happy wherever she was, as long as there was enough to eat and toys to play with. She would sit for hours building with wooden bricks and never cried when Davy knocked her castles and churches flying with one kick of his foot, but would start building them again immediately.

One afternoon when they were all down on the shore of An Tigh Camus, the big white yawl appeared round the southern point of the bay. It was moving slowly in the light breeze from the south, pulled forward by a red and yellow striped spinnaker.

The sight of the striped sail had a peculiar effect on Penelope. She stood up, heedless of Davy's excited chatter. Her heart was beating faster than normally and her cheeks glowed with strange heat as she watched the graceful yacht enter the bay. Its spinnaker was taken down and the other sails were trimmed as it altered course, and making a curve of deeper blue on the surface of the water it swept round the bay and approached the red buoy. Its white sails shimmered and shook as the helmsman brought its bow into the wind.

Standing in a sort of trance, Penelope watched the sails being lowered and stowed away. Then the dinghy was launched and it was when she saw the bright sheen of Hugh's hair as he stepped into the dinghy that she moved. Although every part of her clamoured to stay on the shore and greet the homecomers, she knew that she must not be found there waiting. In that other life she had waited and had held out her arms to a tall man whose hair had been blond, whose cheeks had been bright and whose eyes had gleamed like the serpent's.

Swiftly she swooped on Isa and lifted her in her arms.

'Come along, Davy,' she called. 'Time for tea!'

As she expected, he howled, but she paid
166

no attention, knowing that he would follow eventually. He could not bear to stay alone for long. By the time she reached the lawn in front of the house he was close behind her, wailing that he wanted to see Uncle Tearlach and Hugh.

She stopped walking to tell him that probably his uncle would come to see him later when he was in bed, but by the time she had read three stories and Davy's long black eyelashes were fluttering sleepily on his cheeks, Tearlach Gunn had not come to the nursery and she guessed they would not see him that evening. She felt relieved that this was so because she intended to keep well clear of her employer until Monday was over and her probationary period was over. She was pretty sure that he would not be able to find her unsatisfactory and that she would have the pleasure of seeing him eat humble pie.

Next day from a window in the front of the house she watched the guests leaving. It was the first time she had really had any chance to see them at close range because Tearlach had not considered it necessary to introduce his young relatives to them. One of the men was putting cases into the boot of a car. He turned to say something to someone who was closer to the house and out of her line of vision. Then two women appeared with Kathleen followed by Tearlach. They all stood together with the man laughing and joking obviously facing an unseen photographer. When the photograph was taken one of the women looked up at the front of the house, apparently saying something about it. Kathleen looked up and before Penelope could duck out of sight she had been seen and recognised.

Wishing she hadn't lingered to watch, she scurried away to her own part of the house, not wishing to be caught peeping by her employer. On no account must she blot her copybook this weekend! But where should she go? It being the alternate Saturday, she had the whole day off. She decided that she would find Hugh and ask him about the cruise.

He must have been thinking about her at the same time because half an hour later he arrived at the house to see her.

'I've been hearing from Ian that you have today off,' he said with his inimitable grin. 'So I came over thinking you might like to come to Inverness with me. I'm going to see my mother. Leaving here now, we should be there by one o'clock. We'll have the whole afternoon there and be back on the other side of the strait in time to catch the last ferry at eleven-thirty.'

'I'd love to come,' said Penelope, thinking it was as good a way as any of keeping out of Tearlach's way, and an opportunity to see something of the Highlands.

Soon she was sitting beside Hugh in his old van which rattled round the bends of the road across the island in the pleasant mellow September sunshine. Everywhere fields were showing signs of being ready for harvesting, shimmering with golden light as a faint breeze ruffled the ripened oats and barley. On the moors the bracken was turning brown, but the heather still blazed purple and the rowan trees were aglow, hung with clusters of orange-red berries.

Across the strait of Torvaig the lavender-tinted mountains beckoned beneath a pale blue sky streaked with white cirrus, and Penelope felt a stirring of excitement as she realised that at last she was going to penetrate behind that barrier of rock through the deep glens which delved inland.

As they approached the sheltered fields

of the eastern part of the island she noticed that the reaping had already begun and asked Hugh when he was going to start harvesting his fields.

'I should be starting today,' he replied, 'but I thought to myself that it's also a fine day for driving through the mountains, and there's a young sassenach at the big house with the day off and she hasn't seen much of the Highlands, so I decided the fields could wait another day or two.'

'Supposing it rains?' said Penelope.

'That'll be my bad luck,' he answered with a grin. 'You'll not be saying you're sorry I asked you to come with me?'

'No, I'm glad. Did you enjoy your cruise?'

'It was fine, and an education in more ways than one. I saw the islands of the Outer Hebrides which I've always wanted to visit. We went to the Uists, Benebecula and Barra, and now I know not only how to handle a big yawl but also how to keep at arm's length a woman who has her heart set on matrimony without offending her.'

'Who on earth are you talking about?' demanded Penelope, thoroughly mystified, as usual, by his odd way of referring to events and people.

'My dear sister and the old lion of Torvaig, of course. Who else?' he replied with his wicked grin.

'You mean Mr. Gunn? Why do you call him that? He isn't all that old, although I must say I can see why you call him a lion.'

'He's thirty-seven next birthday, which makes him older than you or I,' retorted Hugh. 'And I call him the lion of Torvaig because the Gunns of Torvaig used a lion's head in their family crest, which you may have noticed is carved over the front door of the big house. And after these last ten days in his company I've another reason for calling him old lion.'

Laughter rippled through Hugh's voice and she turned to glance at him. He was really very attractive, she thought, and she was very pleased to see him again, but sometimes his sense of humour could get out of hand.

'What is your reason?' she asked cautiously.

'I read a story recently in a newspaper. It was about a zoo. The owners of it were having no luck in getting their lionesses to breed, even though they had some handsome young lions. The lionesses wouldn't look at the lions or have anything

171

to do with them. Then one day an old lion was brought from a circus. After years of performing in the ring he had been retired and was going to spend the rest of his life in the zoo. Handsome, yet battered by his life in the circus, he possessed a *je ne sais quoi*, that elusive magnetic attraction which the young lions didn't have, and in no time the lionesses were all over him. Soon the zoo was boasting several litters of lion cubs. After seeing my sister making up to Tearlach during the last few weeks and then watching the two other women on the cruise licking their chops every time he spoke or sat next to them, in spite of the fact that they were both married, I think he's like that old lion. He attracts the opposite sex without any effort at all.'

Penelope couldn't help laughing, although she remonstrated with him.

'That isn't a very nice thing to say about him,' she objected, and he gave her a sharp glance. 'After all, he did ask your sister to act as his hostess.'

'Did he? That's the first I've heard of it. Well, whether he asked her or not she's certainly been trying to turn it to advantage. But his handling of her was very clever and I doubt very much if she knows just where she stands with him now.'

'Mrs. Guthrie is sure they'll make a match of it,' murmured Penelope, who was finding she did not like Hugh's references to his sister's behaviour towards Tearlach.

'I doubt it,' replied Hugh. 'Although Tearlach is probably willing to engage in an affair with Kathleen, I can't see him marrying her. That's why I can't help feeling worried about her. Just lately I've sensed a desperation in her. She's just turned thirty and she has an almost feverish tendency to take anything which might be offered as a substitute for love in the hopes it will be the real thing. I wish I could persuade her to leave Torvaig.'

'Why?'

'I'm afraid she's going to make a fool of herself. As you know Tearlach doesn't suffer fools gladly, and if she throws herself too much at him he might be tempted to discard the kid gloves and teach her a hard lesson in his own rough way, and being very proud and sensitive, she might do something awful as a result. But I didn't bring you with me just to talk about them. Have you blotted any copybooks lately?'

'No, because Mr. Gunn hasn't been near me or his relatives. In fact Davy and Isa might be non-existent as far as he's concerned!' replied Penelope tartly.

'Better keep it that way if it means not making any more blots,' said Hugh with a grin. 'Are you managing the bairns satisfactorily?'

'Of course I am. Davy is still a little difficult. He's so highly emotional.'

'Does he still cry for his mother?'

'Not now. He cries for his uncle instead,' she said dryly. 'Did you ever meet Davy's father?'

'Only once. Davy is very like him to look at. He was handsome, and knew it. He had one of those wonderful physiques which Latin types often have and he showed it off whenever he could, which wasn't often in our climate. But he seemed very fond of Avis, for all she was a bit of a mouse,' murmured Hugh. 'Good, the ferry is in, which means we won't be wasting time waiting for it to come back from the other side.'

The conversation lapsed when they reached the ferry and Hugh had to concentrate on manoeuvring the van across the gangway into the narrow space left by the one other vehicle which was using the ferry at that time. When they started to talk

174

again it was about the sale Ian had made of his entire stock of jewellery to the London buyer and from there it was an easy step to Hugh's own plans to sell paintings which he hoped to make of the scenes he had seen during the cruise.

On the mainland they took the road which led straight from the ferry into the heart of the mountains, following a burn which wound through a narrow glen. Soon they were edging along the shore of Loch Maree, a lovely stretch of fresh water over which the forbidding slopes of Beinn Eighe towered.

The loch was dotted with many islands and Hugh told her that each one had its legend. One of them, known as Eilean Maree, was supposed to be the home of St. Maelrubha, who had founded the church of Applecross, a village on the coast, and the name Maree was in fact a corruption of his name. But in spite of the Christian influence, bulls had been sacrificed in pagan rites as late as the seventeenth century, and a well on the island was credited with curing insanity.

Hugh had many such stories to tell her about the rugged countryside through which the road wound, and the time passed quickly. Enthralled as she had been by the wildness of the scenery, Penelope came back to the amenities offered by modern civilisation with a slight sense of shock as they came down from the mountains to a fertile plain and on to a wider faster road, which took them to the capital of the Highlands, the town of Inverness.

The town was bigger than she had expected, a place of sturdy Victorian villas, many shops and the usual Saturday afternoon traffic. They crossed the bridge over the River Ness, turned blue by reflection, curving away, Hugh said, to the Moray Firth and the North Sea. The steeples of two churches dominated the scene, soaring against a background of houses, factories and the distant hills, tinted ochre by the autumnal sun.

Hugh's parents lived on the outskirts of the town in a gabled granite house. Mrs. Drummond had obviously been on the look-out for them because they had hardly stopped the car in the driveway when a tall slender woman with greying hair appeared at the front door. She came down the steps to greet them and Penelope could see the strong likeness to Kathleen in the lovely lines of cheek and chin and in the amber colour of her eyes. Likeness was also there in the unconsciously regal pose of her head and in the slightly condescending way in which she greeted the nanny employed by her cousin.

'I must say you are as much a surprise to me as I hear you were to Charles,' she said. Her speech was clear and uncluttered by any accent, and Penelope remembered being told once that the people of Inverness spoke the best English in the British Isles. 'I realise now,' continued Mrs. Drummond, 'that Josie Bennet didn't mention your age and I just assumed that she would send an older woman, as I requested. No wonder Charles was annoyed.'

'Penelope looks young and defenceless, but she's well able to take care of herself, and she seems to be doing a better job than Swannie,' said Hugh. 'From all accounts she stands her ground when the lion growls at her and gives back as good as she gets. Today is her day off and I thought you'd like to meet her and see for yourself that Davy and Isa are in good hands.'

'I'm very pleased to meet you, Miss Jones,' said Helen Drummond politely. 'I'm so glad to see you safe and sound, back

177

from your cruise, Hugh. But where is Kathleen?'

Hugh looked slightly uncomfortable as if he didn't care much for having to tell his mother why Kathleen hadn't come with him.

'She wouldn't come. I'll tell you why while we're having lunch. Is Dad home?' he said.

'No. He and Neil have both gone to play golf at Nairn, so unless you stay the night and return tomorrow, you won't see him. It's the closing tournament and of course they didn't want to miss it. Come in, now I'll take you up to Kathleen's room, Miss Jones, and you can tidy your hair there. You'll find the bathroom on the same floor. The meal is all ready and only needs serving.'

By the time she was half-way through the first course of her lunch, Penelope was very much aware that her hostess was an extremely proud and austere woman and that her pride lay in her Highland heritage. Her home was immaculately kept and every piece of the furniture, some of it of antique design, was highly polished. The meal was perfect in every way, excellently cooked and properly presented, with all the right cutlery. It was served in a gracious dining room the window of which overlooked Culloden Moor, that old battlefield where the way of life of the Highland clans had died in a savage fight. Knowing that her own table manners and her whole behaviour were being assessed by those sharp amber-coloured eyes, Penelope could not help thinking of the meal she had taken in the dining room at Torvaig House on the night of her arrival there, and contrasting its casualness with the formality of this meal. No wonder Helen Drummond disapproved of her cousin's way of doing everything. His casual attitude to meals and his disregard for etiquette must have irritated her greatly.

Politely, but insistently, Mrs. Drummond questioned Penelope about her upbringing and her previous job. Penelope answered her coolly and honestly because she had nothing in her past of which to be ashamed. She thought she detected a softening in the other woman's face when she mentioned that her grandmother had been born on Torvaig.

'Then you have a wee drop of Highland blood in your veins, Miss Jones. I'm glad to hear that,' she said with a faint smile.

'More than a little, is my guess,' said Hugh, with a wink in Penelope's direction. 'Ian says Penelope is a true Gael because she has one foot in the past and one in the present, just like you.'

Although Mrs. Drummond raised her shapely eyebrows in mild surprise at her son's use of the nanny's first name, she seemed satisfied by Penelope's credentials and behaviour and turned to the subject which was obviously uppermost in her mind.

'Why didn't Kathleen come with you? I wanted to talk to her.'

Hugh ate several mouthfuls of roast Aberdeen Angus beef before he replied carefully.

'She and Ian are very busy. They are going to hold an exhibition of their work in London in December, thanks to Tearlach.'

'Why thanks to him?' asked Mrs. Drummond.

'He found a buyer for their stuff and is also financing the exhibition. Kathleen came on the cruise with us, but I tell you, Mother, you'll have to do something about her. Either write to her, telling her she must come here for some reason, or go to Torvaig yourself and bring her back here.'

Mrs. Drummond's stiff façade cracked and for a moment she looked thoroughly bewildered.

'I don't mind writing and I'd like to see her, but I'm not going to Torvaig unless Charles invites me, and after our last meeting I don't think he'll be doing that for a long time,' she said with a touch of outraged sensibility.

'Ach, he isn't like that, Mother. He doesn't bear grudges. He says what he thinks, then it's over and he's ready to be friendly again.'

'Well, I'm not like that,' said Mrs. Drummond haughtily. 'I shall never forget the fun he made of all the things I hold dear, the traditions of the Gunn family, handed down through the generations, and which I've tried to preserve because there was no one else to do so.'

'He was only trying to point out that the preservation of those traditions hadn't done him or Avis much good. His father may have been a gentleman like all the other lairds of Torvaig, but that didn't prevent him from not caring a hang for his wife or his children,' argued Hugh. Then noticing the stiffening of his mother's face, he changed his attitude. 'But I'm not here to defend Tearlach. He can do that better for himself than anyone else can. I'm here to tell you that your dear daughter is in danger of making a fool of herself by throwing herself at him. And I think that as her mother, you should do something about it.'

'I shall do nothing of the sort. Kathleen is a grown woman with a mind of her own. She wouldn't like any interference. I don't like Charles, I admit, but if she can get him to marry her, I shall do nothing to stop the marriage from taking place,' said Helen Drummond firmly, and her eyes gleamed between narrowed lids reminding Penelope suddenly of Tearlach Gunn. 'And I hope to see my grandchildren bearing the name Gunn and inheriting the island of Torvaig.'

'Mother, Mother, come out of your tartan twilight,' laughed Hugh. 'The days of arranged marriages between members of the same clan to keep property in the family are over. This is the second half of the twentieth century and to get what they want from each other neither Kathleen nor Tearlach have to marry. There's a distinct possibility that she'll become his mistress. How do you like that?'

This time Mrs. Drummond's expression was one of distaste.

'Really, Hugh, do you have to be so crude? It must come of associating too much with Charles,' she complained.

'I'm not being crude. I'm being frank, as my generation always is about such matters. On the cruise I had the opportunity of watching them at close quarters. Give Tearlach his due, he kept his distance, but the more he plays hard to get the more fascinated and infatuated Kath is becoming. She's at a vulnerable age, Mother, and is just ripe for the picking.'

'Hugh,' remonstrated Mrs. Drummond, 'must we discuss this in such an offensive way in front of Miss Jones? I can scarcely think she is interested in our family affairs.' Then turning to Penelope, she said with a faint smile, 'Let me take your plate. There's fruit pie and fresh cream for dessert. Apples, blackberries and plums all cooked together and placed in the same crust. I hope you like it?'

Penelope said that she did and offered to help to carry the dishes they had used out to the kitchen, but her offer was refused politely yet abruptly, reminding her of the way Tearlach had refused her help when they had been leaving Mallaig in the yacht. In some ways Mrs. Drummond was like him. Both had strong aggressive personalities, but they had grown up in different worlds. The same metal was in both of them, but the manner of forging had been different. She wished suddenly she could see them together, and said so to Hugh.

He shook his head, and said quite seriously:

'You wouldn't like it. Ever heard of blood antagonism? Well, it's there between them. She dislikes him because he's the head of the Gunn family and owns Gunn property, and she doesn't think he is fit to do so. He dislikes her because she wants to preserve all that he hates about the Gunns. You know, she doesn't believe a word I've told her about the possibility of Kath becoming his mistress rather than his wife. She can't accept that a daughter of hers could be so lacking in moral fibre. Talk about a generation gap! I can see it widening between us every minute. You've seen Kath and Tearlach together. You must have noticed the calculating way in which he looks at her sometimes.'

'Yes, I have,' said Penelope.

'Then you can tell Mother, and back me up,' he suggested.

'Oh, I couldn't,' she objected. 'I couldn't tell tales about my employer. That's what Miss Swan did, even going so far as to make up some tales. Once he learned I'd done that he'd sack me on the spot.'

'Ach, I was forgetting your precarious position. But what am I going to do about Kath?' groaned Hugh.

'Why should you do anything? As your mother says, she's an adult and it's her life.'

'I know. If she was dealing with anyone other than Tearlach, I wouldn't worry. I'm afraid she'll do something desperate.'

No more was said on the matter because Mrs. Drummond returned to the room to serve the dessert and for the rest of the meal the conversation was mostly about local activities, including news about Hugh's own nieces and nephew, the children of his elder brother Neil Drummond.

Penelope showed such an interest in Culloden that after the meal was over Mrs. Drummond invited her to go for a walk to the moor, while Hugh called on some friends of his. The moorland, once bleak and wild, was now broken up into fields brilliant with harvest colour and by patches of neatly planted forest.

Together they stood beside the stone

cairn built as a modest memorial to the violent battle and Mrs. Drummond pointed out the long low mounds in the earth which marked where the bodies of those killed had been buried long ago. Each mound was marked by a headstone bearing the name of the clan buried there and, to Penelope's surprise, Mrs. Drummond placed a small posy of autumn flowers which she had brought from her garden on the mound below the rough stone on which the name Drummond could just be seen.

'There is no record of any Gunns being at Culloden, so I remember the battle by placing the flowers on the mound where members of my husband's clan were buried,' she explained to Penelope, and by that single gesture showed more clearly than ever her attachment to the past of the Highlands.

When she told Hugh about his mother placing the flowers on the old grave, he sighed heavily.

'She is one of those who thinks the Highland sun set at Culloden field. She looks back too much. I mean, pride in race and culture are all very well, and I share it to a certain extent, but I'm also aware that you can't stop the clock. Time goes on

186

without you if you do.'

'That's your cousin's philosophy, and also your sister's,' said Penelope, recalling her first night at Torvaig House. 'Maybe that's why they'll gather rosebuds together.'

They did not discuss the subject any more, although it stayed in Penelope's mind to trouble her occasionally during the drive through the mountains back to Torvaig. She found herself recalling vividly the distress on Ian's face when she had told him that Kathleen had gone on the cruise and when he had commented on Kathleen's perpetual presence at Torvaig House during recent times.

Then, quite unexpectedly, she began to wonder about Tearlach's part in all this. Hugh had said his cousin kept Kathleen at arm's length on the yacht, and later had told his mother that Kathleen was becoming infatuated with Tearlach because he kept his distance from her.

Why did he do that? Was it possible he suspected Kathleen's intentions? Did he see the scheming mother behind the daughter, with her eye on his wealth and on his property, that inheritance which Mrs. Drummond regarded as hers? In the light of Mrs. Drummond's approval of her daughter marrying the owner of Torvaig, even though she herself didn't like him, it seemed as if he had every right to be suspicious of Kathleen's advances and to keep her at a distance.

But he was only flesh and blood, after all, and in being tempted to have an affair with her, as Hugh was sure he might be, he could be trapped in an age-old manner and find himself having to marry the lovely woman with whom he had allowed himself to gather rosebuds.

But why should she be worrying about him? The old lion, as Hugh mockingly called him, was wily and worldly-wise, difficult to deceive. Even so she would not like to see him trapped in a loveless marriage, although on the other hand it might serve him right for being so materialistic in his outlook. From all accounts he had not known much love in his life and so possibly he would not know when it was missing from a relationship.

Deep purple gloaming had descended upon the countryside. Here and there a light twinkled from a solitary house, a reminder that there were people living in the apparent wilderness of rock and moorland, through which the remnants of the clans had once travelled, hiding from the red-coated soldiers who had hunted them.

With darkness came heavy cloud. By the time they were skirting Loch Maree, the windscreen was filmed with fine rain. At times visibility was nil and Hugh had to drive slowly, along a road which sometimes hung dizzily over precipices which plunged down to the loch below.

Aware that time was passing, Penelope began to grow anxious. She knew the ferry left Loraig on the mainland at eleven-thirty to take islanders back to Torvaig. It did not return until Monday morning because the strictly religious islanders refused to run it on the day of rest.

'Can't you go any faster?' she asked Hugh. 'I must be in by midnight.'

'Like Cinderella,' he replied with a chuckle. 'I'm doing my best. This fine rain is as bad as mist, and I don't want to have an accident like the one which killed Avis and Manuel. If we miss the ferry, we can always spend the night in the back of the van.'

'I couldn't possibly do that,' retorted Penelope, really worried about being late by now. 'I must get back to Torvaig tonight. Imagine what your cousin would say if I spent the night in the van with you!'

'Mm, I get the point. He's suspicious enough of you and me. We'll just have to hope that Roy Dermid, who runs the ferry, remembers us and holds it back for us.'

His hope was in vain. As the van shot down the final incline towards the Kyle of Torvaig, they could see the lights of the ferry as it sidled across the water. In silence they sat in the van and watched the lights become dimmer and dimmer, and then disappear altogether in the murk.

'I must get back somehow,' said Penelope desperately. 'If I'm not back tonight he'll have every reason for giving me the sack. It'll be a blot I'll not be able to erase.'

'I didn't realise you were so afraid of him,' said Hugh, with a touch of flippancy, as if he couldn't take her plight seriously.

'I'm not. But he did warn me that if I didn't get back by midnight on my days off, there'd be trouble. The least I can do is respect his wishes and remember that he pays my wages, and that when I have time off someone else has to take care of Davy and Isa.'

Respect! The word seemed to mock her. She wasn't afraid of Tearlach Gunn, but she respected him and she would always do her utmost to abide by his wishes.

'I'm sorry, Penelope,' said Hugh contritely, squeezing her arm in the darkness. 'I forgot that it's a question of your bread and butter. Let me think. I should be able to borrow a boat. I'll try Fergus Beath. You stay here and keep dry. You're going to get wet enough, crossing the strait.'

'I don't mind as long as I can reach Torvaig House before Mr. Gunn realises I'm late.'

Hugh was gone much longer than she expected and by the time he loomed up in the dark beside the van she had given up all hope of them reaching Torvaig before daylight. His grin, when he opened the door and told her to get out, reassured her.

'I've managed to borrow a dinghy. Fergus won't come with us because it's the Sabbath now, so I'll have to bring the boat back on Monday. I've launched it and it's tied up at the end of the ferry pier here,' he explained, as they made their way along the pier in the fine seeping rain.

Penelope stepped down into the swaying

191

dinghy after him and sat down in the bow as he had told her to do. The thwart on which she sat was cold and wet and she could feel the damp penetrating her thin skirt. Shivering a little with apprehension, she stared out into the murky night and hoped that Hugh knew what he was doing.

Once the outboard engine had started and the boat was thrusting its way through the inky water, conversation became impossible. Screwing up her eyes, Penelope tried to see ahead, but all she could make out was the flat oily water immediately in front of the bow. Several times she thought she saw the dark sinister shape of a rock looming up and she turned to yell at Hugh, but the shape was only a hallucination after all.

They seemed to have been going for about half an hour when the outboard engine suddenly stopped. The silence was dreadful, accentuated by the lazy lap of water against the dinghy's sides and the pat-pat of raindrops on the calm water. Twice Hugh tried to start the engine, pulling vigorously on the cord while the little boat began to circle round at the mercy of the current.

'It's no use. I daren't waste any more

time trying to start it,' he panted. 'We'll lose our sense of direction if I do. Can you see any light at all?'

He was getting out the oars and fitting them into the row-locks as he spoke. Penelope peered around her. She could see nothing and said so.

'Well, we'll just have to chance it,' he muttered, and sitting on the middle thwart he began to row.

After another half hour Penelope thought she could see light glimmering faintly.

'Let's hope it's the end of Torvaig pier,' said Hugh breathlessly as he rested for a moment. 'The engine should be cool by now. Do you think you could row while I start it?'

Although she had never rowed a boat in her life Penelope could hardly refuse now, when her return to Torvaig depended upon her doing so. The oars felt very heavy and had a disconcerting way of not going in the direction she wanted them to go. After several false starts she managed to get them into the water at the same time, but she had a tendency to 'catch crabs', dipping them in too deeply and flinging up spray which drenched not only herself but Hugh as well.

At last the engine started and with a sigh of relief she slumped on the thwart and pulled the oars inboard. Once more the dinghy bounced through the water, and within another fifteen minutes they could make out the shape of the ferry boat, which was docked at the end of the pier, white and ghostly, beneath the single light which glowed there.

The engine stopped again, but they had sufficient way on to reach the beach, on which the boat grounded softly. Hugh leapt ashore and pulled the bow up so that Penelope was at least able to step on to dry land, where she stood shivering and wet, while he pulled it up further for safety beyond the high water mark.

'Now to find someone who will lend us a vehicle to take us to Torvaig House,' muttered Hugh as they walked up to the road. Not a light showed from any of the houses. It was Sunday morning and everyone was asleep.

'Unless,' added Hugh, hopefully, as they trudged along, 'you'd let me ring up Mrs. Guthrie and ask for someone to come and fetch us.'

'Oh, no, don't do that. I'd like to be able

to get into the house without anyone knowing I'm late,' said Penelope.

'You've got a hope,' he remarked ironically. 'If only Ian was on the phone we could ask him.' He snapped his fingers suddenly. 'I know, we'll ask the Griersons to lend us their bicycles. They're a young couple and not as stuffy as some of the older islanders, so they won't mind if we knock them up.'

When Jimmy Grierson heard Hugh's story he was so amused that he woke his wife Jean so that she could share in the laughter. They agreed to lend their bicycles and Jean wanted them to stay and have a hot drink before they set off. But Penelope was so horrified when she saw that it was two o'clock in the morning that she declined for herself and Hugh, regretfully.

Riding in the dark along the winding road wasn't easy. The connection on the lamp on the bicycle Penelope was riding wasn't very good and so the light kept going out. This meant that she had to depend on the light from the lamp on Hugh's bike, and she had to cycle hard to keep up with him. It was some years since she had ridden, so she tended to wobble all over the road and when they reached a hill the muscles in the backs of her legs ached from pushing on the pedals.

On the other side of the ridge going down towards Torvaig House it was all downhill and they were able to freewheel. By that time Hugh was finding the whole adventure amusing and he put his feet up on the handlebars and let out a series of bloodcurdling Highland yells which split the silence of the wet night, startling the sheep on the hillside and disturbing sleepy birds.

Penelope, who by now was thoroughly irritated with him, managed to persuade him not to come with her to the house, feeling that she could approach it quietly without his help. She left the bicycle under some bushes in the shrubbery. Lights were still on the house, but that was not unusual when the laird was at home because he often left them on all night, forgetting to switch them off when he went to bed.

To her relief the side door was still unlocked and she crept in and along the passage to the back staircase. A light was on there too, and afterwards, when she had time to think about it, she realised that the light and the smell of tobacco should have warned her. But at the time she was so eager to reach her room and go to bed that she did not pause.

Her wet shoes squelched as she walked up the stairs and she could not stop shivering. In fact she felt quite faint with hunger and weariness. She reached the pale green door of her room, opened it and looked straight across the room into the narrowed gleaming eyes of Tearlach Gunn.

CHAPTER FIVE

When Penelope saw her employer lounging at his ease in one of the armchairs in her room, with his feet resting on the coffee table, dismay knocked all the breath out of her and she sank back against the door.

'Oh!' she gasped weakly, as dismay was succeeded by a haze of faintness.

He flung down the book he had been reading, stubbed out his cheroot in the ash tray, stood up and came over to her.

'I ought to give you hell,' he said softly and succinctly.

The viciousness of his attack flashed like a shining blade of a sword through the haze, alerting her, bringing everything back into sharp focus again.

'Why? What's happened? Why are you here in my room?' she challenged.

He placed his hands on his hips and leaned towards her. She cringed back against the door, away from the flare of anger in his eyes.

'I'm here because Isa woke up just after midnight and wanted the potty. I'm here because that woke Davy and he cried because *you* weren't here. It took me an hour to settle him. I'm here, Miss Jones, because you have not been here. I've been doing your job for you,' he hissed savagely.

'But I thought Mrs. Guthrie was looking after them?'

'At midnight Mrs. Guthrie came to tell me you were not back and to ask me what she should do. I told her to go to bed and I would wait for you and listen for the children in case one of them woke up. I've been waiting for three hours. The arrangement was for you to have every other Saturday off until midnight, I believe. Do you agree?' he asked, with suspicious smoothness.

'Yes,' she agreed miserably.

'Then perhaps you'll explain why you're late,' he said. 'I know that you don't think it necessary to account to me for what you do with your time off, but I think when that time off encroaches on my time I can demand an explanation.'

The sarcasm in his voice flayed her. She was tired and wet, and still a little shocked at finding him there, so she said feebly:

'We missed the ferry.'

'Who are "we"?'

'Hugh and I. He took me to Inverness.'

'Why?' It was rapped out and her head reared up in reaction to the autocratic tone.

'He thought I might like to see something of the Highlands and meet his mother. After all, she is responsible for me being here.'

'So she is, blast her,' he said between clenched teeth. 'She's responsible for a lot more too. What time did you leave Inverness?'

'About seven-thirty.'

'Of all the irresponsible, stupid . . .' She guessed he was going to say something rude about Hugh, but he changed his mind. 'He must have known he was cutting it fine,' he went on. 'The last part of the road is hell on a wet night. If you missed the ferry, how did you get here?'

Fighting off the waves of faintness which

were trying to engulf her, bracing herself against the door, she explained in a dull voice what had happened. When she came to the part of the dinghy's engine stopping, he broke in to sneer:

'A likely story!'

That did it. All her resolutions not to let him rouse her temper faded away. She flung back her head and flared at him:

'It's true! You can ask Hugh.'

'And how did you get to the house?' he queried.

'We borrowed bicycles from the Griersons in the village.'

His eyebrows went up and his glance flickered over her wet hair, soaking clothing, down to her wet shoes, as if he'd only just noticed the state she was in. His glance came back to her face, the expression on his face softening slightly.

'Has it occurred to you that your probationary period is almost over?' he asked.

Penelope nodded, feeling her heart sinking.

'I suppose that's why you made an effort to return to the house before midnight? You hoped to get in unseen so that no one would know you'd stayed out after

200

midnight,' he suggested softly.

Again she nodded dumbly in agreement. Her feet felt icy and she longed for a hot bath.

'What's happened to that quick tongue of yours, Miss Jones?' he taunted. 'Lost it?'

'Mr. Gunn, I'm tired and wet and I'd be very grateful if we could postpone the discussion about whether I'm to stay in your employ until tomorrow. I'm sorry I was late tonight. I did my best to get back in time,' she replied, making an effort to appear calm and collected.

'There's really no reason for any discussion,' he said curtly. 'I could sack you now.'

Still braced against the friendly door, Penelope searched frantically in her mind for a suitable retort and found one.

'And save yourself the trouble of having to eat humble pie and take back what you said to me at our first meeting,' she sniped, and to her annoyance he laughed quite easily.

'So you remember that first meeting, do you? Quite a collision, wasn't it?' he said. 'Yes, I could sack you now to avoid eating humble pie, but I'm not going to, because I have something in mind for Davy and Isa

201

which might take a few weeks to come to fruition and it hardly seems worthwhile to sack you and find a new nanny for the short time they'll be remaining here.'

Her amazement at this announcement had the effect of making Penelope forget her own plight temporarily.

'Oh, you're not going to send them away?' she exclaimed.

'My intentions concerning them are merely a few thoughts at the back of my mind and are dependent upon the attitude of other people,' he replied coolly. 'Meanwhile, I'd like to take this opportunity of complimenting you on your handling of them. I admit that when I first saw you I didn't think you were any more capable of dealing with them than Miss Swan was. Added to that your youth created a few complications which we seem to have overcome by having the Guthries to live in.' He paused, and then began to smile. 'There, that's quite a big piece of humble pie for a not very humble person like myself to eat. Does it satisfy you?'

Penelope was never sure what happened next. She was aware of a sensation of relief because he was not going to sack her, which was followed by another feeling of faintness. She remembered thinking that Tearlach Gunn could be very charming when he chose to be and that his smile was enough to make any woman feel faint. Then she was hazily aware that she was being carried to the divan and being placed on it carefully with her head on one of the cushions. Blearily she stared up at him as he leaned over her, an anxious frown between his eyebrows.

'What happened?' she whispered, and in one of those alarming flashbacks she had the impression that he had leant over her like this once before, only then the room had been lit by flaming torches which had cast shadows on the stone walls of a dwelling.

'You fainted,' he said tersely, and sitting down on the side of the divan began to remove her soggy shoes from her feet. 'I'd like to know what Hugh has been up to tonight to let you get into such a state. I thought I'd warned you about him. He's wholly irresponsible and thoughtless about other people. He's been spoilt by his mother.'

'He hasn't been up to anything, and I can't agree with you. He isn't entirely thoughtless. He's very worried about his

203

sister.'

He gave her a narrowed sidelong glance, but made no comment as he removed the second shoe.

'Anyway, it's your fault I fainted,' she continued fretfully. 'You kept me standing about when I was wet, cold and hungry.'

'You can blame me if it makes you feel any better. My shoulders are broad,' he said equably as he placed her shoes on the floor. 'Can you sit up?'

'Yes, of course I can,' she said with a flash of independence. She sat up and the room whirled around her, and the black gulf of faintness yawned before her again. She felt the divan sink to one side as he sat beside her and put an arm round her shoulders to hold her close.

'Steady,' he murmured, and she felt his breath stir her hair. She had a strong desire to stay like that, held against his warm hard body, but his arm slackened and he said impersonally:

'Your jacket is soaking wet. Let me help you get it off.'

When that was done he touched her blouse which was also damp. Beneath the thin stuff her skin seemed to burn in reaction to the feel of his fingers.

'This is wet too. Off with it,' he ordered brusquely.

Alarm that he might help her to take off the blouse too and then proceed to help her take off the rest of her damp clothing cured Penelope temporarily of the faint feeling.

'I can manage, thank you, Mr. Gunn, if only you'll leave the room,' she said coldly.

'Very well. I'll go and warm up some soup for you while you have a bath and change. If you feel faint again just yell and I'll come and help you,' he offered casually, as if he was accustomed to helping women who had fainted in his company.

He left the room, closing the door behind him, and she heard him going across the passage to the kitchenette. Her heart beating frantically she removed her torn stockings, then slipped out of the rest of her clothing. She pretended that the sudden increase in the number of her heartbeats was due to having to move about so soon after fainting, but she had a fear that that wasn't true. Whether she liked it or not, physical contact with Tearlach Gunn had set up a longing within her for more contact, and as she lolled in the warm fragrant bath water, she found herself wishing that she had been conscious when

205

he had carried her to the bed.

She shook her head. What was the matter with her? This crazy light-headed feeling could only be due to lack of food. The sooner she had eaten something and was in bed asleep the better for her. Yet it was pleasant to linger, knowing that someone was finding something for her to eat. He had said he ought to have given her hell for being late, but he hadn't. Oh, he had been brusque and rude, but he hadn't been really angry, and he'd ended up eating humble pie in such a charming manner that all her original antipathy had gone, leaving her with this decidedly odd feeling of wanting to be close to him, to feel his arms around her, his mouth on hers.

The thought shocked her so much that she was up and out of the bath almost before she had realised she had moved. She stood shaking, fighting off the waves of faintness, struggling hard not to give in to the temptation to yell, as Tearlach had told her to do if she felt faint again.

She must be smitten with the same fever as Kathleen Drummond! Hugh had said that his cousin had a way of attracting women without making any effort, and she had thought herself immune!

A loud rap on the door stampeded her into action. She grabbed the towel and draped it round her. She hadn't locked the door and she half expected him to walk in uninvited.

'Are you all right?' he called.

'Yes, oh yes, I'm fine,' she stuttered.

'You've been so long I thought perhaps you'd fainted again,' he said, and she found herself turning pink at the thought of what he might say if he'd known she'd been wallowing in the bath romanticising about him, of all people!

'I'm all right, thank you. I'll be out soon,' she called out, and heard his footsteps retreating.

Back in her room she wished quite irrationally that she had something more glamorous to wear than the simple blue pyjamas and blue woollen dressing gown, suitable for wearing in the night when attending to crying babies. Then she doused the thought with a shower of common sense. He probably wouldn't be interested enough to notice what she was wearing.

Entering the kitchenette, from which came the tantalising smell of hot soup, she went across to the table and sat down in one of the chairs quickly as grogginess threatened once more to overwhelm her. Tearlach heard her and turned to look at her searchingly.

So much for thinking that he wouldn't notice what she was wearing, she thought, as she braved his narrow gaze which took in everything from her tousled dark hair to her serviceable leather slippers.

'This soup smells very good. I think I'll join you in your early morning feast,' he murmured. He crossed to the table with two bowls of smoking soup, set them down and then sat opposite to her.

She had never known a simple meal of canned soup and toasted bread taste so good and she wondered whether her taste was affected by the company she was keeping at that hour of the day. At no time in her life had she shared a meal with a man in the small hours of the morning.

Across from her sat the one who had prepared the meal and who had very recently helped her when she had fainted. In his own way he had been kind and surprisingly gentle. Having had to cope for so long by herself with the few illnesses she had known she appreciated his help. Yet for the last month she had been regarding him as a heartless ruffian incapable of a kind thought, let alone a kind deed. How differently he appeared under the present circumstances!

He had finished his soup and was leaning back in his chair seemingly lost in thought. Looking at him, Penelope noticed for the first time that there was humour as well as shrewdness and cynicism in the lines around his mouth and eyes. There was also confidence and strength in his face, and those who are confident and strong can afford to be gentle, she thought.

He looked up suddenly, smiled and said:

'Do you feel any better?'

'Yes, thank you. Much better.'

'Good. Then perhaps you won't mind if I go back to what I was saying before you fainted,' he continued in businesslike tones. 'You seem to go down well with Davy and Isa and can cope with them satisfactorily. I'd like you to stay on here until their future is settled. Will you do that?'

At this point in time when he looked at her like that she was willing to do anything he asked, thought Penelope dreamily. Anything!

'Yes, of course,' she murmured.

209

'Even though it will mean you'll probably be looking for another job in another household around the end of November?' he queried, giving her a shrewd glance.

She did not like the sharp pang of disappointment which stabbed through her at the thought of having to leave Torvaig so soon, but she covered it up by saying coolly:

'Changing jobs is something which nannies always have to keep in mind. May I ask what you intend to do with the children?'

'I think you are aware that their father was not British,' he said.

'Miss Swan told me that.'

'My sister met Manuel when he was attached to the Spanish Embassy in London. She had gone to London to work, and they met at a party. When they decided to marry apparently his family were horrified. She was not considered good enough for him. In spite of their objections, Manuel went ahead and married her, and his father refused to have anything more to do with him.'

'How mean of him,' murmured Penelope hotly, her eyes sparkling with her dislike of such injustice. 'Have you met him?'

'Yes. He came to Manuel's funeral after the crash, but was unable to stay and see the children. Since then I've been in touch with Señora Usted, their grandmother. It seems that she's coming to Britain in a few days' time on her way back from South America. She's travelling with her daughter. I've invited them to come to Torvaig to see Davy and Isa. They should be here by the end of October.'

'If they couldn't come when your sister and her husband were alive, how is it they can come now?' demanded Penelope. 'They seem very hypocritical to me.'

His mouth twisted wryly in appreciation of her remark.

'Let me explain their attitude a little further. As far as they were concerned my sister was a nobody, a typist in an office, like dozens of other girls in London. The Usteds are a very ancient family as well as being wealthy. Honour and pride of race count for everything with them,' he said.

'As they do with some Highlanders,' commented Penelope, thinking of Helen Drummond.

He grinned at her.

'Now I know you've met Helen,' he said.

'Anyway, it seems that the Usteds are much more disposed to accept an invitation from Avis's brother, who happens to be the owner of an island in Scotland and is apparently descended from Highland chieftains, and who at the same time holds considerable shares in a certain oil company in Venezuela in which Señor Usted is also involved. Money talks, Miss Jones,' he added cynically.

'I'm beginning to realise that. But what has this to do with Davy and Isa?'

'Reading between the lines of the letters I've received from Señora Usted, I have the impression that she was very fond of her elder son and would like to have the upbringing of his children in her hands.'

'Will you let her take them to Spain?'

'If I'm satisfied that they'll be well-treated and will be given a good home, I shall.'

'But you promised your sister that you'd take care of them,' objected Penelope.

He looked suddenly very troubled, the lines etched on his face deepening as he rubbed his hand across his forehead, pushing the hair from it. In Hugh the same gesture was boyish, attractive. In Tearlach it was one of weariness of spirit and it

212

touched Penelope's heart in a way that didn't happen when she saw Hugh do it.

'I know. She didn't know what she was doing. She hardly knew me,' he muttered. 'I suppose she thought she was doing the best she could for them.' He glanced up at her suddenly, his eyes wide and for the first time she saw that they were blue, darkly blue. 'I can see you don't approve of what I intend to do,' he accused harshly.

She straightened in her chair.

'It isn't my place to approve or disapprove of what you wish to do,' she said stiffly.

He banged the table with the flat of his hand.

'Come off it, Miss Jones. You've disapproved of me ever since we met because of my materialistic outlook on life, and you haven't hesitated to tell me so. I thought you'd be delighted to think that Davy and Isa might find a home with someone who can give them all the love they're lacking here.'

'Would that be your only reason for letting them go to Spain?' she asked.

'What other reason could there be?'

'I thought perhaps that you were considering marriage and that the children would be an inconvenient encumbrance to you and your future wife,' she replied.

His face stiffened and his eyes narrowed to those dangerous gleaming slits which always made chills run up and down her spine.

'A good try,' he jeered. 'Who put you up to it, Helen or Hugh?'

He must think she was prying on behalf of his cousins to find out if he was going to marry Kathleen. Indignation that he should think that brought Penelope to her feet.

'No one did,' she snapped at him.

'Then you should remember that whether I intend to marry or not is my affair at the moment and no one else's,' he rapped back. 'I've discussed the matter of the children's future with you, because as you're employed as their nanny, it naturally involves you. I'd be obliged if you don't mention the possibility of Señora Usted's visit until I'm sure she is coming. As soon as the harvesting is done, I shall go down to London to meet her and the Señorita, and shall escort them back here if necessary.'

Still quivering from the reprimand he had delivered, Penelope bent her head and looked at her hands.

'Yes, Mr. Gunn,' she muttered.

He stood up and came over to her. To her surprise he put a hand under her chin and forced her to look up at him.

'I know you look very pretty when you are being meek, but I also realise that it's a pose as unnatural to you as being humble is to me,' he scoffed. 'I think I prefer you when your cheeks are on fire, your eyes are flashing blue sparks and your tongue is spitting flame at me.'

'Oh, you are the most—' she began, and got no further, for his hand moved upwards and clamped over her mouth. Over it she glared up into eyes which were suddenly brimful of laughter.

'I agree with you entirely,' he said, 'but calling me names isn't going to change me. Now, can you make it to bed under your own steam or would you like me to carry you there again?'

Using all her strength, Penelope wrenched free of his restricting hand, gave him one more glare and then fled from the kitchenette, through the sitting room to the bedroom, and banged the door closed. Her heart thumping loudly, she waited. Nothing happened. He didn't follow her, and as her heartbeats slowed down, she wondered why she had thought that he would.

She heard the door of the kitchenette being closed and then the creak of a board on the landing as he went past to the stairs. Only then did she untie the belt of her dressing gown, fling it off and climb gratefully between the cool sheets of the bed to fall asleep almost instantly, exhausted by her nocturnal adventures.

*   *   *

Three weeks later Penelope stood on the headland looking down into the bay. It was empty. No big yawl swung at its mooring on the periwinkle blue of the water. It had gone to the mainland, taken at the beginning of October by Tearlach and Hugh to be laid up in its winter quarters. Even the red buoy had gone.

She sighed a little before turning away to continue her walk across the headland to Cladach. The big house was also empty again. Oh, the children and the Guthries and she were still there, but the laird was away, gone about his business in the city. He had been gone almost a week now and when he returned at the beginning of

November he would bring Señora Usted and her daughter with him.

And from the moment of their arrival Penelope's days on Torvaig would be numbered. This thought, which recurred often, distressed her far more than it should because since the night of her return from Inverness she had woken every morning with a wonderful feeling of contentment. Her period of probation over, she felt settled in the big house on the island of her dreams, close to the place where her grandmother had been born.

She had felt particularly secure while the owner of the island had been there and she could see him going about the estate consulting with various workers, helping with the harvesting on the Home Farm and occasionally coming to talk to her and the children.

But now the harvest was over. All had been safely gathered in during a spell of fine weather, and the fields lay shorn under the pale skies and slanted sunlight of October. Tearlach Gunn had left the island and so had Kathleen Drummond.

It was said by Ian that Kathleen had gone to London to see the buyer who had bought all their stock of jewellery and who would

217

be organising the exhibition of their work in December.

Hugh, however, had a slight different tale to tell when Penelope had called on him and had found him absorbed in his painting, making an effort to record the images of the past summer.

'She may be seeing the jeweller, but you can guess who else she's seeing,' he had growled. 'She and Tearlach are probably staying at the same hotel in adjoining rooms.'

Penelope hadn't liked what he'd said, so she'd pushed it to the back of her mind. It had an unpleasant way of pushing to the front of her mind on afternoons such as this one, when the sea was a placid lavender colour and the distant islands were finely etched against the autumnal sky and the Hebridean tranquillity gave rise to feelings of nostalgia and yearning.

Afraid of those feelings, Penelope turned from the view and was soon on the road, which curved round the edge of Cladach Bay, on her way to Achmore and Ian.

He wasn't in, so she walked up the hill to the graveyard. As usual it was quiet there. Only the occasional bleat of a hillside sheep or the plaintive cry of a whaup winging slowly over the moorland disturbed the peace. Once again the past came around her as she peered in at the chapel window. She was the slave wife of the first Magnus Gunn waiting to meet the hermit priest to discuss the best way of converting her heathen Viking husband to Christianity.

The priest wasn't there, but she could see him coming up the lane, brown-haired and bearded, with sandals on his feet.

Penelope blinked rapidly and the priest became Ian, just turning in towards his house. Shaking off the past, she hurried down the hill and entered the workshop soon after him.

'I've had another flashback,' she said. 'Between us we converted Magnus Gunn to Christianity.'

He smiled at her, his usual warm welcoming smile, but she noticed that his face was drawn and sad. Beneath his eyes were lines, scored by sleeplessness.

'And that's the way it was,' he murmured. 'The heathen Norsemen soon adopted the Christian faith of those they had conquered. Some of their festivals were absorbed into the church year, just as some of the Celtic festivals were also adapted to Christianity. In fact we shall soon be

219

celebrating the great Celtic fire-festival held in honour of the sun.'

'Which is that?' asked Penelope.

'Hallowe'en, on the last night of October. The fire-festival was always held on the last day of the ancient Celtic year. The new year always began in Scotland with the entry of winter on November first. At dusk the Druids lit great fires of sacred wood on the hilltops and offered up sacrifices, partly as a sort of thanksgiving to the benevolent sun which had ripened the crops, and partly for purification and protection from the powers of evil during the dark winter months to come.'

'What form will the celebration take on Torvaig?'

'I expect there'll be the usual dance and children's parties, ducking for apples and so on. I believe Hugh is concocting something with Molly Lang, but he'll tell you all about that himself,' said Ian with a touch of weariness, as if he couldn't be bothered with childish amusements. 'Let's go over to the house. I have something to show you which we found in the dig. We'll put the kettle on and have a wee *strupach* together. I'm glad to see you. I'm tired of working and just lately the days have been long and wearisome.'

'Are you missing Kathleen?' asked Penelope. 'Have you heard from her?'

'Yes, I do miss her, and I haven't heard from her, neither has Hugh. Any news of the laird?' he replied, opening the door of the house and gesturing to her to go in.

'No, he won't be back until the first of November,' she said. Then, made anxious by the stricken look on Ian's face, she rushed on into the kitchen. 'I'll make the tea and you find whatever it is you want to show me.'

In the small neat kitchen she busied herself taking out crockery, making far too much noise as she did so, humming to herself and occasionally breaking into song, trying to pretend that Ian did not look unhappy. And all the time in her mind she was talking to Kathleen Drummond, telling her what a fool she was for throwing herself at Tearlach Gunn and saying that Ian McTaggart was worth two of the laird, then contradicting herself and saying no, he wasn't, but he was different.

Ian was gentle, idealistic, a bit of a dreamer, with one foot in the past like herself. He needed someone practical and hardheaded to look after him; to see that he

221

ate the right food at the right time and didn't spend too many hours bending over his silver work. Whereas Tearlach was tough and realistic and didn't need anyone to look after him.

When she went into the living room with the tray, Ian had just come downstairs. He had changed his mud-stained clothes and in his hand he was carrying something wrapped carefully in tissue paper. He put the small parcel down on the table and carefully unwrapped the paper. There, gleaming on the white softness, was a brooch. It was circular in design, and made of gold. A pin made of the same metal, which had a carved head was attached to the brooch.

'It's beautiful!' exclaimed Penelope.

'It is a superb piece of craftsmanship, a pennanular brooch which would be worn by a man to secure his cloak, and the inscription on the back is in Norse,' said Ian, turning the brooch over and showing her the markings round the circle.

'What does it say?'

'I think it says "Magnus owns this brooch,"' he replied. 'As soon as Tearlach comes back I'm going to ask his permission to let me take it to a museum in Glasgow to have it verified. The carvings on the front of it I'm sure are Celtic in design, not Nordic, and I think it's another example of the fusion of Celtic and Nordic races and culture, which took place not only in the Highlands and the Hebrides but all over the British Isles in the early part of the ninth century.'

As he talked some of the weariness left Ian's face and, noting this, Penelope led him on to talk more about the artefacts he had found.

Outside the sun slipped down behind the dark silhouettes of the Outer Isles and inside they switched on the lights to disperse the gloom as they talked. Then Penelope made a simple meal for both of them and later Ian walked part of the way back with her in the cool October night which held just a hint of frost.

They came to the other side of the headland and paused to look down at the dark water of the bay in which the sickle of the new moon was admiring its own reflection.

'When the moon is full it will be Hallowe'en,' said Ian with a sigh. 'The year is going fast, and I had intended to do so much before it ended.'

'Such as?' prompted Penelope.

'Such as asking Kathleen to marry me,' was the surprising reply. 'I hoped that once success came my way I'd be in a position to ask her. Success, to a certain extent, has come. I have more orders for jewellery than I can cope with, but Kathleen seems to be lost to me,' he said mournfully.

'She's only in London,' replied Penelope.

'And probably with Tearlach,' he said heavily. 'I can't bear to think what he'll do to her, not deliberately because I don't think he's a cruel person, but unwittingly because, being invulnerable himself, he does not understand how easily others can be hurt.'

'Why don't you go to London too?' urged Penelope. 'After all, you have a perfectly good excuse for going. You could say you wanted to know what was happening about the exhibition.'

He turned to her and to her surprise touched her gently on the cheek.

'You are kind, and sensible too, and I value your friendship. This afternoon I was as low-spirited as a man can be and you came, to sing in my kitchen, make my tea and laugh me out of my misery. It's no wonder children love you. I would go to London, but I hate big cities and I'm afraid

224

of what I might find there. It's better if I stay here and wait. One day Kathleen will have need of a friend and she'll remember and come running back to me.'

Penelope was about to remonstrate with him, but he touched her cheek again and said:

'No, don't tell me I should have more courage and should be prepared to go out and fight for my love. I'm not a knight in armour ready to go and slay dragons. I can only sit and wait. Good night, Penelope. Come and have tea with me again.'

*　　*　　*

The autumn days drifted by. Life went on quietly. Davy and Isa helped Penelope rake leaves from the lawn and then played in the heaps they had made, or helped Alec Guthrie to plant bulbs for next year's show of spring flowers.

No word came from the laird and no word from Kathleen, as Penelope discovered one day when Hugh turned up to see her and was sent upstairs by Mrs. Guthrie to the bed-sitting room where it often seemed to her the smell of cheroot smoke still lingered, and a small slender book on sailing lay on the coffee table waiting to be returned to its owner.

'I'd no idea you were so well done to,' said Hugh, looking round with a grin before he collapsed into an armchair. 'It certainly pays to be a nanny these days,' he added, reaching out and picking up the book from the table. He glanced at the title, flicked open the cover and stared at the fly-leaf. Knowing what was written there, Penelope watched him and held her breath.

He whistled softly, cocked an eyebrow at her and read the written words with a questioning lilt in his voice.

'Charles Gunn, eh?'

She met his slightly mocking gaze squarely.

'He left it the last time he was up here,' she said coolly.

'And when was that?'

'The night we missed the ferry.'

'You mean he was waiting here for you at three o'clock in the morning?' He sounded incredulous as he placed the book back on the table.

To her intense irritation Penelope's memory, over which she seemed to have no control, winged back to the time she had returned to her room, tired, wet and hungry, and had fainted into her

226

employer's arms, and a tide of pink colour washed over her face. It was noted by Hugh's mocking eyes.

'I thought you'd managed to get in without being seen and that was why you didn't get the sack,' he murmured. 'I wonder what it is that Tearlach has which makes such a big impression on women? He hasn't always been pleasant to you, yet the mere thought of him has made you blush and his presence in London has kept my sister Kathleen down there long after she should have finished her business there.'

'Have you heard from her?' asked Penelope, refusing to let his reference to her blush embarrass her.

'No. Neither has my mother, although of course she isn't at all worried as she thinks her little plan to get her own back on Tearlach for having the audacity to come back after all those years and claim as his what she thought should be hers may work yet, and her daughter might become mistress of Torvaig!'

Penelope moved restlessly about the room, startled by his reference to a definite plan on Mrs. Drummond's part. She did not like to think that Tearlach Gunn might fall a victim to his older cousin's machinations.

'Any news of when Tearlach might return? It would give me some idea of Kath's movements,' asked Hugh casually.

'The first of November.'

'Good. Then that means we mice can have another play,' he said with a chuckle. 'Are you going to come to the Hallowe'en dance in the village hall?'

'How can I? It's on a Friday and you know my time off is on Wednesdays and Saturdays.'

'You could swap one Wednesday for a Friday, I'm sure. Mrs. Guthrie would oblige. Will you ask her? It's going to be fun. Molly Lang and I have been thinking that some of us might dress up as witches or ghosts, like we used to do as children, and call on people all over the island before we go on to the dance. At each house we'll sing a song or recite a poem.'

'Sounds like fun,' said Penelope. 'I'd like to come.'

'Then be at Molly's house on Wednesday night. We're all going to meet there to make plans.'

Penelope did as he had suggested, going first to Ian's house to watch him working in his workshop and then to have tea with him. He didn't mention Kathleen once and she thought he seemed much more relaxed than the last time she had visited him. She was quite surprised when he told her he was going to the dance and would be taking part in the guising which Hugh and Molly had planned.

They went together to the Langs' house and it wasn't long before the meeting to discuss costumes and masks had turned into a *ceilidh* as Hugh suggested songs that they might sing and played them on his guitar and they all sang. Disguises presented no problems because the men were all going as ghosts, wearing old sheets, and the women as witches in black paper hats and cloaks. Masks were to be made by the women.

While she was at Molly's house Penelope received an invitation for Davy and Isa to a children's party which Aileen Guthrie was organising for little ones on the afternoon of Hallowe'en, at which they would duck for apples and play other games.

When the last day of October came it was damp and mild, the sea flat and grey, stretching away to a faint horizon. Davy and Isa enjoyed the party at the Home

Farm and Penelope had no trouble in settling them for the night as both children were tired by their activities.

Penelope had not been to many dances in her life. This was the first time she had ever been sure of having a partner. Ian would be there to escort her and to show her how to do the intricate Scottish dances, so it was with a flutter of excitement that she dressed in a long blue and white patterned skirt which she teamed with a white lace blouse. The blouse had a low neckline gathered with a drawstring which tied in a bow between her breasts. Over this outfit she wore a short coat and then the black witch's cloak.

Hugh was late coming for her and she was sitting in the kitchen wearing the high black hat on her head and holding the white and red witch's mask, talking to Mrs. Guthrie, when they both heard footsteps coming along the passage from the direction of the front hall.

'It must be the laird,' exclaimed Mrs. Guthrie, rising to her feet. 'He's come earlier than I expected.' She went to the door, opened it and called out, 'Is it yourself, Mr. Gunn?'

'It is,' came the answer, and Tearlach

appeared in the doorway. Above the black high-necked sweater which he was wearing under his black and white tweed jacket his face was pale and slightly drawn, and he frowned against the bright lights of the kitchen.

As he saw the small dark form crowned by a tall black hat holding a hideous mask in front of its face, his eyes narrowed suspiciously.

'Who's that?' he demanded of Mrs. Guthrie.

'A wee witch who dropped in on her way to the Hallowe'en dance which is on in the village hall tonight,' replied the housekeeper, her eyes twinkling with mischief behind their glasses.

'And how is she going there? By broomstick?' queried Tearlach dryly. He crossed the room and lifted the high hat off Penelope's head.

'I thought so,' he murmured, as she looked up at him, her mist-blue eyes wide, her cheeks a dusky pink and her heart knocking against her ribs in reaction to this unexpected encounter.

'I changed my day off so that I could go to the dance,' she said defensively.

The smile which always began in his eyes

widened his mouth and he dropped the hat back on her head.

'You're going with Hugh, I suppose,' he said.

'And Ian, and the Langs and the Griersons,' she said hurriedly, not wanting him to think she was going alone with Hugh. Quickly she explained what they were going to do. Hands in his pockets, his head slightly bent so that his blond streaked hair fell forward on to his forehead, he watched her expressive face and listened. When she had finished talking it seemed to her that he looked rather wistful, almost envious, as if he would have liked to have been participating in the evening's fun and merriment. With a sudden impulsive wish to erase that expression from his face, she said urgently:

'Please come to the dance.'

For a moment, there in the kitchen from which Mrs. Guthrie had gone, they looked at each other as equals. She was no longer his employee. She was a young woman going to a dance and he was the man she had invited to go with her. The differences which had always existed between them created by age, outlook and background were as nothing. Their minds met and were

232

briefly united.

Then the horn of a motor vehicle sounded brashly outside. Mrs. Guthrie bustled into the kitchen to say Hugh had arrived and the moment of brief union was over. A bland shuttered expression came over Tearlach's face and he turned away, said something to Mrs. Guthrie and went quickly from the room.

The horn sounded again, Penelope grabbed her broom and her mask, and hurried down the passage to the side-door, wishing with all her heart that Hugh hadn't come just then and that she wasn't going to the dance with him and the others.

Outside the night air was cold and damp and a hazy moon was peering down out of a black sky. As soon as she was settled in the van beside Hugh, Penelope sensed there was something wrong.

'Where's Ian?' she asked.

'He isn't coming.'

'Why?'

'Kathleen came back on Wednesday evening. I tried to persuade her to come with us tonight, but she dismissed the whole idea as childish and wouldn't come. I didn't want to leave her alone, so Ian said he'd stay with her.'

Penelope was silent, looking out at the dark shapes of the land, thinking back to the taut tired paleness of Tearlach's face when he had appeared in the kitchen and wondering what had happened between him and Kathleen in London.

'The laird is back too,' she said at last.

'I saw his car,' murmured Hugh.

'Did he teach Kathleen a lesson?' she asked diffidently.

'Yes, but not in the way I expected. From what I can make out from her rather sparse comments he didn't take much notice of her. They met only once and that meeting was not very pleasant,' said Hugh tersely.

Penelope experienced a strange surge of relief.

'Is Kathleen upset?' she asked.

'I think so. Of course, I can only judge by her behaviour. I haven't done anything right in her eyes since she came back, and poor Ian has really been suffering from her sharp comments.'

'I'm sorry about that,' said Penelope. 'I know he was hoping she would need him.'

'She does, but she won't admit it. As far as she's concerned, all men are now to be regarded as no good, just because Tearlach

234

showed that he couldn't care less about her. You see, he ignored her because he was far more interested in another woman who was staying in the same hotel.'

'Oh.' Penelope was so surprised she couldn't think of anything else to say.

Somehow after hearing about Tearlach's treatment of Kathleen and his involvement with another woman, she found it difficult to be as gay as the others as they went from farmhouse to farmhouse, and croft to croft, singing their songs and accepting their treats offered to them in the old time-honoured way of celebrating Hallowe'en. They reached the village hall soon after ten o'clock, but even though the dance was in full swing, Penelope felt slightly out of the gaiety and she spent many of the dances sitting alone and watching.

She told herself that she would have felt differently if Ian had been there. He would have been her partner. She could hardly expect Hugh to stay with her all the time because she knew that, being a naturally gregarious person and fond of dancing, he wanted to dance with every woman who was present in turn.

The odd feeling that she had sat like this and had waited for someone to arrive once before swept over her suddenly, and she turned to glance in the direction of the main entrance to the hall. With a sense of shock, she saw Tearlach standing near the door talking to some of the young men who worked on the estate. He had changed into Highland dress, which accentuated the blondness of his hair and the freshness of his complexion and drew attention to the strong line of his jaw. While she watched, the Scottish country dance band took the stage again and sounded an introductory chord. The master of ceremonies announced a group of dances which would be played, and dancers began to form sets on the floor. Tearlach looked round as though searching for someone. His glance alighted on Penelope, sitting in the corner by herself, and he began to shoulder his way through the crowd towards her.

He stood in front of her, an apologetic expression on his face.

'I don't dance,' he said bluntly.

'I can't dance this sort of thing,' she replied.

'Then we'll sit out together and watch,' he said, and promptly sat down next to her.

'Why have you come?' she asked.

He gave her a long lingering glance

which took in her shining dark hair, faintly flushed face, white-skinned neck and shoulders and the blue bow nestling between her breasts.

'If any other woman had asked that question I would conclude that she wanted me to answer "Because *you* asked me to come, darling",' he said, with a touch of mockery. 'But because it's you who asks I have to tell you I'm not sure why I came, just as I'm not sure whether you invited me to come or whether you were merely making a suggestion that I should come because it's the sort of thing I should do as laird of Torvaig. As a matter of interest, which was it? An invitation or a suggestion?'

He was no longer pale or tired-looking and seemed full of that vibrant energy she would always associate with him.

'I don't know,' she answered a little wildly, confused by his nearness. 'It just came out. When I was telling you what we intended to do tonight you looked wistful, as if going out guising on Hallowe'en night and then going to a dance was something you'd always wanted to do and never been able to do, and suddenly I wanted to share the experience with you.'

'As Nanny Jones or as the reincarnated wife of the first laird of Torvaig?' he jibed lightly.

'Oh!' She swung on him to retaliate scornfully, saw the glint in his eyes and recognised it as amusement. 'I'm beginning to realise that you needle people deliberately to provoke them into retaliating,' she snapped.

He laughed outright.

'And I've a feeling you're beginning to get my measure, Penelope Jones, because you're quite right, I do.'

'Then you can't have many friends,' she said crossly.

'That's true, I haven't, but those I have seem willing to put up with my needling, as you call it. Tell me, have you enjoyed yourself this evening? Has it been an experience worth sharing? It seemed to me you looked a little forlorn sitting here in the corner all alone,' he commented.

He must have been watching her before she had seen him, and she wished that she had been in Hugh's arms, dancing with wild abandon, when he had arrived.

'No, I haven't enjoyed it as much as I had expected,' she admitted reluctantly.

'Because Ian isn't here?' he asked

shrewdly. He leaned back in his chair and placed his arm along the back of her chair in an effort to be more comfortable on the hard narrow seat.

'Partly. He was to have been my partner,' she said.

'Why didn't he come?'

'He wanted to stay with Miss Drummond instead.'

'Why did he want to do that?' he asked, with a lilt of surprise.

'I don't suppose *you*'ve noticed, but he's in love with her.'

'No, I hadn't noticed, because, unlike *you*, I haven't a romantic slant on life and don't go round looking for such behaviour. Does Kathleen know he's in love with her?'

'He's never told her, but she should know by now, because he preferred to stay with her tonight to comfort her instead of coming here.'

'Why does she need comfort?' He asked the question idly as if he were only half interested in the conversation.

'You should know,' she challenged. 'I would have thought that you of all people should know why she came scurrying back to Torvaig and why, now, all men are an anathema to her.'

He glanced at her sharply.

'That's strong language you're using,' he mocked softly. 'You sound as if men are anathema to you and that's why you can sympathise with her. Why should I know why she's been behaving oddly? I ran into her a couple of times in London. One night when I'd been out to dinner I returned to find her waiting for me in my room. I had some difficulty in explaining her presence to my business associates as well as to Señora Usted, who being Spanish has some very definite views on the way a young unmarried woman should behave. Kathleen could have become an embarrassment, so I had to tell her that although she is my cousin I really didn't have the time to take her out and about, as she seemed to expect.' Penelope looked at him. His face wore a bland expression, but there was an amused twinkle in the depths of his blue eyes. Exasperated by that twinkle, she sat up straight and said with a touch of acidity:

'You know very well why Kathleen is miserable. She's in love with you, and you've encouraged her by letting her supervise the furnishing and decorating of your house, by allowing her to act as a hostess to your guests. She had every right to think you wanted to be more than a cousin.'

The twinkle vanished. The eyes that returned her accusing glance were hard and cold.

'I'd always managed without a hostess until she got it into her head that she would look beautiful sitting at the end of the dining table by candlelight, or reclining gracefully on the deck of a yacht,' he observed cynically.

'You took her to Edinburgh, too.'

'That was her idea, too,' he murmured. 'You're on the wrong track this time, Miss Romantic Jones. Kathleen is not and has never been in love with me. She has been in love with the idea of herself as the wife of the owner of Torvaig. She has been encouraged in that by her mother, who is convinced her side of the family has more right to the island than I have, and has done her best to poke a finger into my pie ever since I returned to Scotland. She pushed her daughter forward to help me with the doing up of the house and later to act as a hostess when I had guests. She provided me, very conveniently, with an old friend of hers as a nanny for my sister's children

241

when they were left in my charge. And when I managed to get rid of that nanny because I suspected her of spying on me and taking her tales back to Helen, she was only too pleased to offer to find me another nanny.'

Penelope flashed him an uncomfortable glance. He was watching her with narrowed eyes.

'Is that why you wanted to send me back to London? You thought I was going to spy on you?'

'Yes, especially when I noticed how friendly you were with Hugh. I'd hoped to put off the new nanny by going for her in a sailing boat, but the weather let me down. Then you stood up to me and answered me back so honestly that I began to think perhaps I was wrong in my suspicions of you. I let you come on probation and warned Hugh to stay away from you, then waited to see if you were going to spy on me on behalf of Helen. You put yourself completely in the clear the night you returned from Inverness, much to my relief. I wouldn't have liked to have sacked you, when you were obviously very good at your job. As for Kathleen,' he added with a slight shrug of his shoulders, 'Helen should have known better. I'm not a callow youth to be bowled over by the approaches of a beautiful woman with seduction in her mind.'

Penelope sat still and straight. A reel was being performed and the floor was shaking with the beat of many feet. She was glad Tearlach had not been taken in by Helen Drummond's little plot to ensnare him as a husband for Kathleen, but she kept thinking of Ian who had been made extremely unhappy by recent events.

'Ian is welcome to Kathleen,' said Tearlach suddenly. 'She is cold and proud like her mother, and I can't help thinking he would do better with someone like you, a little impulsive, but sound at heart. Have you fallen in love with him? Is that why you were looking all forlorn a few minutes ago?'

The question surprised her and she sat silent, examining her thoughts on the subject. Was she in love with Ian? Had she fallen in love with him because he was the exact opposite to Brian who had hurt her? Was that why she went often to his house and sat with him and made his tea? Utterly confused by her own feelings, she could find no answer to Tearlach's question.

A hand tugged her hair back hard and

kept on holding it.

'Come on, give. Are you in love, as you call it, with Ian?' demanded Tearlach. Although his voice was rough there was laughter in it too, as if the whole idea of people falling in love was highly amusing. His amusement irritated her and she refused to add to it.

'I'm not going to tell you,' she retorted, twitching her head so that her hair was pulled from his hand. 'You won't torture me into telling you my secret feelings, even if you do pay my wages.'

'Fair enough,' he replied equably, just as the music ended and groups of laughing, breathless dancers began to make their way to the chairs set round the side of the hall.

He stood up and leaned over her.

'I'm going to take you home,' he said firmly. 'The way Hugh is carrying on, you'll never get back to the house before midnight. Go and get your coat and I'll see you outside.'

Before she had a chance to reply and refuse to go with him, he turned and walked away. She saw him stop and have a few words with Hugh, who glanced across at her and nodded his bright head with a grin and a wink, showing that he had agreed that she should leave the dance with his cousin.

Not sure whether she wanted to be taken home by her employer, she went to the cloakroom, slung her coat over her shoulders, put on the tall hat, collected her broomstick and went outside, through the back door of the hall.

The sky had cleared and the moon was high, silvering everything with its radiance. In the nearby strait the water glittered and on the mainland she could see the mountains silhouetted against the sky.

On the grey asphalt of the car park behind the hall her shadow appeared before her, grotesque and elongated. A witch carrying a broomstick. If only she could really ride it all the way back to Torvaig House, and avoid the intimacy of the front seat of a car being driven through the night.

As she walked round the end of the hall to the road she wondered whether she could find Hugh's van and hide in it until Tearlach gathered that she didn't want to go with him and left without her. But her wild plan was short-lived, because he was standing by the front entrance of the hall, waiting for her, and as soon as he saw her he came towards her.

'I thought you'd gone by broomstick, little witch,' he murmured, taking her arm and guiding her inexorably towards his car.

'I would have done if I could,' she replied, and he laughed.

'Let this be a lesson to you. Never invite a man to a dance unless you're prepared to let him take you home afterwards,' he jeered softly, and she stiffened with alarm. 'Here, put your broom and hat in the back seat and come and sit in the front with me.'

Reluctance showed in every movement she made as she did as he directed. Soon the car was sweeping with a muffled roar along the single village street. Then the open road was before them, a path of ghostly grey leading to the mysterious darkness of the moors.

CHAPTER SIX

In front of Tearlach's car, Penelope sat looking out at the moon-bleached road and thought about Ian and Kathleen, together in Hugh's little cottage on his croft at Cladach Bay. Were they also looking out at the moon? Were they holding hands after

Ian had confessed his love? Perhaps they were kissing. She had no doubt that Kathleen would accept and return Ian's love once she had been told about it, and that their story would end happily, as all true love stories should.

'I brought Señora and Señorita Usted back with me today,' Tearlach's quiet yet vibrant voice broke into her romancings, bringing her back to reality with a jolt.

'How long will they be staying?' she asked.

'That will depend to a certain extent on the weather. Being used to a warmer climate they won't take kindly to the sort of weather we have up here in November. It will also depend on how the Señora takes to Davy and Isa,' he replied crisply.

'And how they take to her,' she couldn't help saying.

'That too, although it isn't as important because they're both too young to have a say in the matter. They'll do as they're told,' he retorted curtly.

'Poor little things,' she said softly.

'You needn't be too heavy-handed with the pity,' he countered. 'Señora Usted is extremely fond of children and apparently doted on Manuel. It was against her wishes that Señor Usted would have nothing to do with his son after his marriage, and she thinks she could have talked her husband round into accepting Avis, eventually. Unfortunately before that could happen they were killed. The accident upset Señor Usted very much and now he wants to do all he can to make it up to Manuel's children—a natural enough reaction.'

Penelope didn't say anything. What could she say? He didn't want the care of the children and he was doing his utmost to get rid of them.

'It's just possible,' he went on, 'that Señora Usted will be interested in employing you when she sees how well you handle them.'

'I'm sure she'll prefer to employ a Spanish nanny who could manage equally well, and would have the advantage of being able to teach them to speak Spanish,' she replied shortly.

'It would save you the trouble of having to look for another job. Why not keep it in mind?' he returned practically.

'I've no doubt that it would ease your conscience considerably, Mr. Gunn, if Señora Usted took me away with her as well as them,' said Penelope tartly. 'You can't

248

wait to be rid of them, can you?'

'It isn't a case of wanting to be rid of them,' he answered coldly. 'I have to do what I think is best for them, and what I think Avis and Manuel would want for them. I'm convinced they will have a much better home with Señora Usted than with me. Also, since Davy is the only son of the Usteds' eldest son, he stands to inherit considerable wealth and property.'

'What about love? Will they inherit any of that?' asked Penelope, wondering why she disliked him to talk in this way about the children.

'You are hung up on that word love, aren't you? You've been on about it ever since you came to Torvaig. Tonight it was, "Ian's in love with Kathleen," and Kathleen's in love with me. I think it's just another word for sentimentality,' he jibed as he swung the car round a bend far too fast for Penelope's comfort.

'That's because no one has ever loved you, and as a result you have never loved anyone,' she flung at him, hurt by his mimicry of her. 'Do you want Davy and Isa to be as deprived as you have been?'

He was silent, and she guessed, with a feeling of uneasiness, that this time she had scored a hit where it hurt him most. She had breached the wall behind which he hid his real feelings. But she derived no pleasure from the fact. Instead she was overwhelmed by a desire to apologise. The words formed in her mind, but were never spoken, because fear closed her throat as a dry stone wall loomed in front of the headlights and she was convinced the car was going to hit it.

The wall fell away to the left as the car skidded round the bend and roared through the night down a straight stretch of road. Tense on the edge of her seat, Penelope searched for the safety belt, managed to fasten it, and then leaned back with her eyes closed.

'Do you have to drive so fast?' she objected in a husky voice at last.

The car slowed down immediately and from then on his careful handling of it as he took it round the last few bends was a deliberate insult to her.

'Were you frightened?' he asked.

'Yes,' she whispered.

'I intended you to be, because there are times when you irritate me so much I come very close to wringing your neck,' he said viciously.

'I know, I'm sorry,' she quavered. 'After the children, I come next on your list of people you'd like to be rid of. I wouldn't be a bit surprised if that isn't why you've thought up this plan to push your responsibility for them on to someone else. Then you won't have to employ any more nannies.'

'You never give up, do you, Penelope Jones?' he said through gritted teeth. 'All right, have it your way. Although that aspect of letting the children go to live in Spain had never occurred to me, now that you mention it, I agree. The relief in knowing that I won't have to put up with a self-righteous little prig who has spent her time trying to change me will be enormous. A good riddance.'

Penelope felt vanquished. Had she really seemed like that to him, a Mary Poppins of a nanny trying to change the ways of her materialistic employer? She had no retort ready and sat slumped in her seat, wishing with all her might that the drive was over; wishing she'd never given in to impulse and invited him to the dance. As Molly Lang had once said, Tearlach Gunn was a hard nut to crack and in trying to crack him a woman could destroy herself. Kathleen

251

Drummond with all her beauty had failed and had returned to Torvaig bruised. Why should Penelope think that she, a plain little nobody of a nanny, had any better chance?

They turned into the driveway and in a few minutes the house appeared, grey and ghostly in the moonlight. Wishing to be ready to leave the car as soon as it stopped, Penelope began to unfasten the safety belt, but by the time the car had stopped in front of the house she was still struggling to release the clasp of the belt, which seemed to be jammed.

Tearlach switched off the engine and the lights, then noticing her furtive, desperate fumblings he turned towards her.

'What's wrong?' he asked irritably.

'The clasp on the safety belt won't open,' she admitted reluctantly.

He leaned towards her and his hand touched one of hers as he felt for the fastening. Already in a highly emotional state, she reacted wildly snatching her hand away and jerking backwards as if from a snake bite. In the moonlight which slanted in through the windscreen she saw anger glinting in his eyes as he looked at her.

'What the hell's the matter with you?' he

growled. 'I'm only going to try and release the fastening for you. Or would you rather I didn't? I could quite easily leave you to struggle on your own. I don't pretend to be chivalrous, although I don't mind helping people, if I think they need help.'

She leaned further away from him, back against the door, her face chalk white in the light from the moon, her eyes pools of darkness.

'I give you a bad time of it, don't I, Penelope?' he said in a softer voice. 'Once I made you faint. Tonight I frightened the wits out of you because I drove too fast, and now I've reduced you to a jelly-like state just because my hand happened to touch yours. I think it's high time I gave you something to shake about.'

His hands grasped her shoulders and she was pulled roughly against him. His mouth came down on hers in a savage kiss which sent desire shooting through her, flame-like, consuming all resistance to him. There was silence in the car, broken only by their quickened breathing. It stretched into minutes as, finding so little opposition to his goodnight kiss, Tearlach settled down to enjoy it, relaxing against the back of the seat holding Penelope closely.

Warmed and comforted by his hold, she let him have his way, responding freely, twining her arms around his neck to keep him close, while the curious moon slid reluctantly down the sky and soon had its view of what was happening in the car, hidden by a discreet and kindly cloud.

It was the opening of the front door and the spilling out of light on to the front steps, followed by the crunch of footsteps on the gravel, which brought them both to their senses. Pushing her away from him, Tearlach sat up, thrusting a hand through his hair to push it back from his forehead, and turned to open the window on his side of the car.

Mrs. Guthrie approached and bent her head to peer in.

'I thought I heard a car. Is it yourself, Mr. Gunn?'

'No one else, Mrs. Guthrie,' he replied, with a touch of mockery. 'I've brought Miss Jones home from the dance.'

'Ach, well now, that's just as well, because Davy has just been sick, the poor wee soul. He can't stop vomiting and I don't know what to do with him.' She looked past Tearlach to Penelope, who was doing her best to tidy her hair and her clothing, hoping that her lipstick wasn't smudged and that she didn't show any other signs of having been made love to quite extensively. 'Perhaps you'll come to him straight away, miss. He'll feel better as soon as he sees you. You know how much he misses you when you're not there. He's had too many green apples at the party this afternoon, I shouldn't wonder.'

'I'm coming, Mrs. Guthrie,' said Penelope breathlessly. 'Good night, Mr. Gunn. Thank you for bringing me home.'

'The pleasure was mine, Miss Jones,' he replied, not bothering to control the amusement he was feeling. 'Wait. You can't go yet. You're still fastened in.'

Once again she felt his hands moving against her as he fiddled with the clasp and she held her breath until it was unfastened and he moved away.

'Good night,' he said coolly, as she opened the door. 'I hope Davy will be recovering by morning, because I shall want to see him to tell him about his visitors.'

* * *

The possibility of Davy being in a fit state

255

to see his uncle the next morning became more and more distant as the night wore on. It seemed to Penelope that the little boy vomited every half-hour, and she gave up lying in bed to go and sit in the armchair in his room, so as to be on hand. Twice she had to change his bedclothes and she soon decided that his sickness wasn't due to green apples as Mrs. Guthrie had suggested, but was caused by a germ. Her experience with that sort of stomach upset had taught her that nothing could be done until the vomiting had stopped.

In a way she was glad to be busy most of the night because she knew that she had been able to go to bed she would have lain awake a long time, wrestling with her thoughts. Even so she still had time to think between Davy's bouts of sickness, although she tried hard to keep thought at bay by reading a novel.

But the events in the car before Mrs. Guthrie had opened the front door were too recent and too real to be obliterated by fiction, and as she relived them Penelope kept wondering what would have happened next if Mrs. Guthrie hadn't opened the front door when she had.

Her cheeks suddenly hot with

embarrassment, she could not help feeling slightly shocked at her own behaviour, and the heat in her cheeks increased when she thought of how amused Tearlach must have been by her passionate and easily aroused response to his punishment. He might not have loved or have been loved, but he certainly knew how to make love. All the time she had known Brian he had never been able to rouse her in that way and she had thought she had loved him.

At last Davy fell into an uneasy sleep and, curling up in the chair under the eiderdown she had brought from her own bed, Penelope slept too, worn out by the discovery she had made about herself that night.

She was awakened after less than three hours' sleep by Isa crying and vomiting. She hurried to the little girl's room. Feeling jaded and suspiciously squeamish herself, she changed the sheets on the cot, washed the little girl and put her in clean nightclothes, then sat down beside her, all prepared to do for her as she had done for Davy during the night.

Before morning had progressed very far she realised she also had the stomach germ, and leaving Isa during a lull, she crept

257

down the stairs to tell Mrs. Guthrie.

'Ach, you poor soul!' exclaimed the housekeeper, although it seemed to Penelope, who was still feeling guilty and miserable about her behaviour in the car the previous night, that there was a reproachful glint in Mrs. Guthrie's eyes. How much had she seen last night before Tearlach had heard her, and had moved? How long had she been standing beside the car?

The questions twisted through her mind, unanswered.

'I'd be glad if you could explain to Mr. Gunn,' she said. 'He was going to come and see Davy and Isa this morning and then bring the visitors to see them, but I think it would be better if they all stayed away from the nursery until we're better.'

'I'll tell him. But is there anything you're wanting now?' asked Mrs. Guthrie. 'Shall I ask the doctor to come?'

'No, it won't be necessary. Davy is already sleeping it off and I should think Isa will be over the worst by midday. If you'll just warn Mr. Gunn, I'd be very grateful.'

At that point Penelope had to turn and run, as she felt a wave of nausea sweeping

258

over her.

The morning was one of the worst she had ever known in her life. Between her own bouts of nausea she had to get up and attend to Isa and then to Davy who, although he had slept, was petulant and wanted her to stay with him all the time. She had just ordered him rather weakly to go to sleep again and had lain down on her own bed when the door of her room opened and Tearlach walked in.

'I hear you're not well,' he said, coming over to the bed and looking down at her. Conscious of her tousled hair and greenish-white cheeks, she stared up at him. He looked full of good health and energy, his cheeks bright, as if he had just enjoyed a walk in the frosty air, and his eyes gleaming between narrowed lids.

'I'll be better soon,' she said, and tried to smile, but to her horror tears of self-pity brimmed in her eyes and rolled down her cheeks.

'Not if you keep on having to get up and down to those two, you won't be better soon,' he remarked dryly, as Isa screamed to her to come and at the same time Davy let out a fretful bellow that he wanted a story reading to him. 'I've arranged for the doctor to come,' continued Tearlach, 'but until he arrives I think you'd be better off in another bedroom away from the kids.'

'No,' she objected as forcibly as she could.

'Yes,' he retorted, with a sudden heart-jolting smile, which made her feel weak, only in a different way. 'Now don't argue with me, there's a good girl. I know you're very conscientious and all that about your job, but this is one time when Davy and Isa can do without you. Can you manage to walk or shall I carry you?'

He spoke as if carrying her from one room to another was a normal procedure. Penelope imagined the expression on Mrs. Guthrie's face if she saw the laird carrying the nanny in his arms through the house, and sat up quickly and swung her feet to the ground. She stood up and nausea attacked her immediately.

'No, you mustn't carry me,' she managed to mutter, and then added hurriedly, 'I think I'm going to be sick again.'

'Go ahead, don't mind me,' he said mildly. 'I'll wait for you and have a word with that abominable nephew of mine, who sounds as if a good spanking wouldn't do him any harm.'

When she emerged from the bathroom Davy had stopped yelling and Isa was quiet. Tearlach was waiting in the passageway. He took her by the arm in an impersonal way, although as soon as he touched her all sorts of strange sensations tingled through her, in spite of her feeling ill.

'Come on,' he urged. 'Mrs. Guthrie has put an electric blanket in the bed, so it should be warm by now, and you're to stay there until I tell you to get up.'

'But what about your visitors?' she asked.

'They're no concern of yours,' he said curtly.

'But who'll look after the children?' she asked.

'Never mind. For the next few hours you've to think only of yourself and to concentrate on getting well again.'

He took her down to the second storey of the house where she knew the other bedrooms were. The room he led her into was big and pleasant, decorated in a colour scheme of wine-red and grey. Sunlight streamed into it through two windows which overlooked the bay.

Penelope stood uncertainly by the double bed which looked inviting with its freshly-laundered striped sheets turned back to reveal firm pillows. She was waiting for Tearlach to leave the room before she took off her dressing gown. But it seemed he wasn't going, because he stood there waiting too.

Eventually, with fingers that fumbled, she untied the belt and unbuttoned the shabby gown. As she tried to slip it off he stepped behind her and lifted it from her shoulders so that she had only to pull her arms out of the sleeves. Very conscious of her thin cotton pyjamas, she hurried to the bed and slid between the warm sheets while he placed her gown on the chair near the bed.

'Does that feel better?' he asked, coming to look down at her.

She nodded, suddenly shy of him. Then she said what was uppermost in her mind, faint colour creeping into her wan cheeks as she remembered how closely he had held her in the car the previous night.

'I hope you don't get the germ.'

'I hope not too,' he replied, and there was a suspicion of a smile in his eyes. 'The doctor should be here soon. Is the sun bothering you?'

'No. I like to see it, thank you,' she said politely. The delicious warmth of the bed was making her feel drowsy already, and she was having difficulty in keeping her eyes open.

'I like it too,' he murmured. 'That's why I have my room on this side of the house.' But she hardly heard him, nor did she feel him push her hair back from her brow as he murmured, 'Sleep well.'

★ ★ ★

She slept so well that she never heard the doctor come into the room. According to Mrs. Guthrie he refused to disturb her from such a sound sleep, deciding that it was a far better cure than any he could offer.

The housekeeper had come into the room in the late afternoon and had awakened Penelope when she had closed the window.

'How are Davy and Isa?' was Penelope's first question.

'Ach, they're getting along fine, just fine.'

'Have the visitors seen them?' was the

next question.

'Aye, they have that,' said Mrs. Guthrie with a touch of enthusiasm. 'There's no doubt that the Señora is a lovely woman. When the laird told her that perhaps she ought to wait until they were well before she saw them, she overruled him like a true grandmother and went straight to the nursery to give them the gifts she had brought. Wee Davy took to her at once. Ach, you can say what you like, uncles and aunts are all very well, but when you haven't any parents, your grandmother is the next best person, as both you and I should know.'

'Yes, I do know,' said Penelope, but she could not help her heart from sinking. If Davy liked his grandmother so much he would soon be leaving Torvaig, and so would she.

'What about Señorita Usted? Is she nice too?'

'Aye. She's a wee bit older than yourself, very pretty in a dark foreign way. She's been out all afternoon with Mr. Gunn looking at the island. Alec had a wee crack with her this morning when she was looking round the gardens. He says she's very knowledgeable about plants,' enthused Mrs. Guthrie.

'I'm sorry to have been such a nuisance having to stay in bed like this,' murmured Penelope. 'I think I should get up now.'

'Mr. Gunn says you've to stay there until he sees you again,' said Mrs. Guthrie firmly. 'It wouldn't be so bad if all the spare rooms weren't in use and you could have gone into one of them.'

Penelope looked round the room wildly, noting for the first time that it didn't have an unused look that spare rooms usually have.

'Whose room is this?' she demanded weakly.

'Himself's. Whose do you think?' said Mrs. Guthrie, with a glint of disapproval. 'I never thought I'd see the day when an employee would be sleeping in the laird's bed. But them I'm learning that Heather Swan was right when she said some funny things went on in this house and that Mr. Gunn was a bit unconventional in his ways.'

'I can't stay here,' said Penelope urgently. 'I must go back to my own room.'

She flung back the covers and was about to step on to the floor when Tearlach appeared in the open doorway.

'You'll stay where you are,' he ordered brusquely. 'The doctor said you wouldn't be fit to work until the day after tomorrow. You've had one of those twenty-four-hour stomach 'flu germs. Make the most of your time in bed, because you might find yourself having to look after the rest of us.'

Realising that there was no point in arguing with him when he spoke like that, Penelope lay back in bed and let Mrs. Guthrie cover her up, which the housekeeper did with much clucking of her tongue and many warning flashes from her bright eyes.

'But what will you do? Where will you sleep?' she managed to ask at last.

'Downstairs in the study. There's a bed-settee down there. I just came to get a few articles I need from the drawers here,' he replied. 'Do you feel like eating?'

'No, not yet.'

'Then that settles it. In bed you stay until tomorrow.' He was opening and closing drawers, and when he had found what he wanted, he came to stand by the bed and smile down at her.

'Stop worrying about it,' he admonished gently. 'It's my reputation which will suffer, not yours. Isn't that right Mrs.

Guthrie?' He flung a narrow suspicious glance in the direction of the housekeeper.

'Not if I can help it, Mr. Gunn,' replied the housekeeper, although she looked rather troubled. 'I'll away now to see that the table is laid in the dining room.'

She bustled out of the room, leaving the door wide open.

'It was mean of you to say that to her. She's quite upset at the idea of me being in your room,' said Penelope. 'She thinks the world of you, and now it looks as if you're wilfully destroying her good opinion of you. Couldn't I have gone into another room?'

'Only if I'd asked Señora and Señorita Usted to share a room,' he said, 'and I wasn't prepared to do that. I suppose as laird I'm expected to turn a blind eye when one of my employees is sick, just because she's a young woman and the rest of the household might get the wrong idea about her morals as well as mine,' he added, with a bitter twist to his mouth. 'I didn't have the advantage of being brought up as a gentleman, like my father, and I know nothing about love, as you do, but I do care when anyone is ill or is in trouble, and I try to do something to help. I do what I feel is best at the time, not what I'm *expected* to do. But I thought you'd understand that, because you usually do and say what you feel instead of what you think, don't you, Miss Jones?'

Was he referring to last night when she had returned his kisses with passionate interest, or was he referring to all the times she had told him what she felt about his attitude to life? She was too confused to tell and could only blink up at him.

'Obviously you're not on form or you'd have come back with some provocative remark designed especially to prick my inflated ego,' he murmured, with a wicked grin. 'I'll leave you to rest now. Don't worry about Davy and Isa. They're having a great time with their granny from Spain.'

He left the room, banging the door closed behind him, and Penelope was left alone to reflect on the fact that she was no longer needed at Torvaig House.

Although by the next afternoon she felt fully recovered, she found that the children were quite contented to stay with their grandmother and aunt and did not require her supervision. At a loose end, she decided to have some fresh air and she walked over the headland to Cladach to see Hugh.

She found him in his studio flinging paint at the canvas. She was sure that the mess he was making was the ultimate in self-expression, but she hadn't the slightest idea what the various blobs and swathes of colour were supposed to be.

'You could have knocked me down with a feather when I saw Tearlach at the dance the other evening,' said Hugh. 'Then, when he told me he'd come to take you back to the house, I wondered what was wrong.'

'He doubted your ability to take me back before midnight. You have to admit you slipped up the last time you took me anywhere. Hugh, what is this painting about?'

He gave her an exasperated glance and then grinned.

'Do you mean to tell me that you don't recognise it? That's Torvaig as we saw it the day you came to the island. Stand back and you'll see the bay, the rocks and the lighthouse. If you try really hard you might even see the spirits of Magnus Gunn and his Irish slave wife.'

She stepped back and gazed hard at the picture. In the cold northern light coming through the window all she could make out were wild sweeps of reddish-brown which she assumed were land, a flat wash of yellowish-grey, which she supposed was the sea, and a stark, upright streak of white, which she guessed was the lighthouse.

'I can't see the spirits,' she complained, with an impish grin, and he proceeded to chase her round the room with a paintbrush dipped in orange paint. He only stopped threatening to paint her face when she gave in and admitted that the painting did resemble the view of An Tigh Camus from the sea.

'Why all this sudden activity?' she asked, strolling round the studio to peer at other canvases. 'Who's this?' she exclaimed, not waiting for an answer to her first question.

'Molly Lang, of course. Who else has hair that colour?' he replied.

'But she isn't cross-eyed. She has just a slight cast in one eye.'

'That's how she looks to me,' replied Hugh serenely. 'And the answer to the first question is that the date of my exhibition in Edinburgh has been brought forward and if I don't do some painting I'll have nothing to exhibit.'

'Where is Kathleen?' asked Penelope,

suddenly aware that his sister wasn't in the house.

'Striding about the moors somewhere, like a tragedy queen. She's all taut, angry and silent. I'm quite afraid she'll do a Lucy of Lammermuir one of these days and start screaming at me,' murmured Hugh, sitting on his stool once more and applying paint to his picture.

'Who's Lucy of Lammermuir?'

'Don't you know the story about the girl who went mad at her wedding? One of Sir Walter Scott's best. Donizetti made an opera out of it. A real hair-raiser.'

'But why should Kathleen do that? Because your cousin gave her the cold shoulder in London?'

'Possibly, although I'm thinking there's something more to it than that. She and Ian aren't speaking to each other at all.'

'Oh. I thought he'd have told her he loves her by now,' said Penelope, disappointed.

'He might as well have come with us for all the good he did by staying with her on the night of the dance. She went off to bed and he sat here all alone.' A thought occurred to him suddenly and he stopped painting to swing round and stare at her. 'It

271

isn't Wednesday· or Saturday, it's Sunday, so what are you doing here?' he asked.

'We have visitors.'

'Ach, yes. Kath recognised them when she saw them with the laird yesterday. The young one is the woman in whom Tearlach showed so much interest in London.'

'She's Davy's Aunt Rosa and the other woman is his grandmother from Spain. They've come to see the children with a view to taking them back to live in Spain with them.'

Hugh whistled soundlessly.

'It's a pity they couldn't have come while Avis and Manuel were alive,' he said.

'That's what I think, but never mind, they're here now, and the Señora is more than willing to make amends for what happened in the past.'

'How long are they staying?' asked Hugh.

'A week, maybe two. Then I think they'll probably take Davy and Isa with them to Spain.'

'Tearlach will be relieved if they do. He never saw himself as a beneficient guardian. But what will you do?'

'I don't know yet. Señora Usted has offered me a position in her home to continue as their nanny, but I'm not sure.'

'What does Tearlach say?' Hugh regarded her curiously.

Penelope thought back to the conversation she had had that afternoon with her employer and from which she had not yet recovered.

'*He* thinks it would be the chance of a lifetime for me. The Usteds are wealthy and live in a beautiful place on the shores of the Mediterranean Sea. They know all the *right* people and have all the *right* contacts, whatever that means,' she replied scornfully. '*He* thinks I should go with them.'

'Then why don't you?'

'Because I don't want to leave Torvaig. I'd like to go on living here. I feel right here.'

'Have you had any more flashbacks?'

'Yes, when I lived here before I had children. Boys, strong and golden, like young lions.'

'Why, Penny Jones, you're becoming quite poetical,' he scoffed. 'Who was their father? The old lion of Torvaig House?'

'Hugh Drummond, you should be—' she began, and then realised there was no mockery in his eyes. He was looking at her quite seriously.

'How do you know?' she demanded.

'The way your face changed when you looked up and saw him at the dance,' he replied, applying more paint to his picture. 'He brought you here in his boat and you've lived like a servant in his house. At first you hated him, but now you're going through a period of not being sure. That's why you don't want to leave.'

In a panic because Hugh with his observant artist's eyes had noticed more than he should, Penelope paced about the room. Hugh swung round again and watched her.

'It's one of those physical things,' she flung at him, by way of explanation. 'Women have them just like men. I'll get over it.'

'Supposing it is? There's nothing wrong in that. In fact I always think that purely spiritual love between a man and a woman must be damned dull. I know of a way in which you could stay on Torvaig.'

'How?' she asked.

'You could claim one of the crofts at Achmore and live on it.'

'But I'd have to plough the land and grow crops and look after animals, and I

274

know nothing about those things,' she said slowly, thinking how much she would enjoy owning and working a croft.

'You'd soon learn. Many women in the islands look after the crofts and you'd be following the tradition of the Viking women who enjoyed good status, owning their own land and managing their own property,' replied Hugh. 'It would be better than working as a nanny all the time, belonging nowhere and to no one.'

His suggestion appealed to Penelope's imagination. Already she could see herself independent and free.

'Where will I find out about the croft?' she asked.

'You'll have to ask Tearlach himself. He probably knows all the legalities about proving that you're Hector Sandison's only descendant. Of course, these days you don't even have to do that if you really want a croft and there is one available, but the fact that you have a right to one here gives you more pull, should he say he doesn't want you to have it.'

'Most of the other croft owners do some other sort of work,' murmured Penelope. 'There isn't much I can do except look after children.'

'You can take in tourists in the summer. There isn't really enough accommodation on the islands for visitors. Tearlach has often mentioned that it's time there was a hotel or even a youth hostel. Oh, there's plenty of possibilities for anyone who is willing to work,' said Hugh.

During the next week, when she was supposed to be considering the position offered to her by Señora Usted as nanny to Davy and Isa when they went to live in Spain, she kept thinking about the last remaining empty house on the hillside above Ian's croft. Maybe it was right that she should go and live there and till the ground, and become part of Torvaig's community. She had no ties, no relatives to make claims on her, and during the past few weeks she had made friends whom she knew she would value all her life. Why leave them when she could stay?

In the end she decided that there was only one person whom she could ask for advice on the matter. She would have to talk to Tearlach himself about it. She would let him make the decision for her. If he said no, he didn't want her to have the croft which was hers by right, she would abide by his decision knowing that he had meant what he had said on Hallowe'en night, that she was a prig and that he would be glad to be rid of her.

His criticism still hurt, even though she knew he had been goaded by her criticism of him into flinging such words at her. They hurt almost as much as the memory of his lovemaking in the car did. There had been an undercurrent of contempt to the way he had kissed and fondled her, as if he had known the effect he would have on her because he had been able to set other women afire with desire, and he considered she was no better than they had been.

And she had to agree with him, she wasn't any better than Kathleen Drummond, who was beautiful and proud yet had gone chasing after him to London. Nor was she any better than Rosa Usted, who was gay and highly intelligent yet stayed downstairs long after everyone else had gone to bed to talk with Tearlach alone in the lounge or in his study.

One afternoon Rosa, whose English was excellent, brought the two children back to the nursery for their tea and asked if she might stay and have the small meal with them.

She was a well-made young woman of

medium height with a mop of waving black hair and a plump olive-skinned face. Her smile was wide and friendly, a curving of full red lips over white slightly crooked teeth. She wore little make-up and was dressed that afternoon in a wine-red sweater and beautifully-cut tweed skirt.

'I would like to see what you give them to eat,' she explained. 'It is important, because at first we shall try to give them the food they are accustomed to and then gradually introduce them to Spanish food. We don't want their small tummies to be upset too much.'

Penelope showed her how to poach two eggs and serve them with fingers of hot buttered toast. Rosa decided she would also have a poached egg and soon she and Penelope were having tea together in typical British fashion.

'This is very pleasant,' said Rosa. 'I would like to think you are coming to Spain with us, Miss Jones, but I think that is not so.'

Penelope looked up in surprise and met a pair of very shrewd twinkling black eyes.

'What makes you think that? Señora Usted gave me until Friday to make up my mind, and I haven't decided yet.'

'If you really wanted to come to Spain you would not be taking so long to come to a decision. It isn't often the chance comes the way for someone like you, who has to work for her living, to go to Spain to live in the sunshine away from this horrible climate.' She glanced with a shudder at the window which was being lashed with rain and shaken by the wind. Then she looked back at Penelope with an apologetic smile. 'You must forgive me,' she said, 'if I'm critical of the weather, but it is as you say, the end.'

Penelope laughed.

'Yes, I'm afraid it must seem like that to someone who isn't used to the damp and the cold.'

'Perhaps there are other attractions that I don't know about which make you want to stay here?' suggested Rosa with a sly little smile.

'How do you know I want to stay here?' countered Penelope.

'You walk about this house with a confident manner as I do in my parents' home, as if you belong here, and then you talk to Charles as if you had known him a long time and will go on knowing him an even longer time,' replied the Spanish girl, still watching Penelope closely.

Alarm shot through Penelope. This intelligent, very pretty girl noticed far too much.

'Possibly it seems like that to you only because he and I are of the same race and culture. I've only been here two months and I haven't known him longer than that,' she replied cautiously.

The Spanish girl raised her eyebrows in slight surprise.

'One would not think so,' she murmured. 'But you do want to stay here and not come to Spain. Am I not right?'

Suddenly Penelope found herself confiding to Rosa all about her grandmother and the Sandison croft. Rosa listened with interest and said finally:

'I understand about the croft. Charles has taught me much about the Highlands since I have been here. It is very exciting that you can own your own land. You must talk to Charles soon, before you give my mother your decision. Then if it isn't possible for you to have the croft you will still have the chance to come with us.'

Rosa paused and a faint enigmatic smile flitted across her face.

'I hope our return to Spain will not mean

the end of our association with Charles,' she continued. 'He is very charming. He took me about London. I find him much more relaxed than the younger men with whom I usually go about. But then he is not impressed by my father's wealth and so is not intent in making an impression on me. We deal very well together.'

Too well for Kathleen's peace of mind, thought Penelope. She had noticed how attentive Tearlach had been towards the Spanish woman and had occasionally been appalled at the flashes of jealousy she had felt as a result.

She asked Hugh whether he thought his cousin was attracted to Rosa when she saw him again the next afternoon. He had met the Usteds by this time and so was able to pass an opinion.

'After seeing them together the other evening I think there's a possibility that he is attracted to her. After all, his sister and her brother were so attracted that they were willing to defy the Usted family,' reflected Hugh. 'But then Tearlach is a wily old lion. He gave the impression that he was attracted to Kathleen too and deceived all of us. He's not above putting on an act, you know.'

'For whose benefit?' snapped Penelope.

'Anyone who happens to be noticing. You, for instance,' he said, with a mischievous grin, 'so that you won't get any ideas above your station.'

'Oh, if you're in that sort of a mood I'm not staying any longer,' retorted Penelope. 'I'll go and see Ian and make his tea. At least he's too civilised to mock.'

'Yes, do that,' replied Hugh, his face suddenly grave. 'He's pretty miserable these days and would welcome a visit.'

Ian was interested in the possibility that Penelope might stay at Achmore and he suggested that they should walk over to the croft. They found the stone walls of the little house still sound, but that they would be improved by being rendered and painted white on the outside. The roof was in a bad state and needed recovering.

'If you ask Tearlach he'll get someone to see to that for you,' said Ian. 'Most of the houses round the bay here were in the same condition, and look at them now.'

Inside the house was a different story. There was no doubt in Penelope's mind that a great deal of work would have to be done to the interior of the walls before she could live in the place.

'I shall look forward to having you as my nearest neighbour,' said Ian in his deep slow voice. 'If you would like to earn a little extra cash during the winter I'd be glad if you'd come and clean my house once or twice a week and perhaps do some baking for me.'

'But what about Kathleen?' asked Penelope.

'She'll be leaving Torvaig,' he said with a sigh. 'After the exhibition she'll be setting up her own workshop in London nearer to the market.'

'Oh, I'm so sorry, Ian. Why didn't you tell her?'

'There was no point. She was looking at me and talking to me, but not seeing me. My little dream concerning her is over just as hers concerning Tearlach is over too. We're both a little sadder and a little wiser.'

'I still think you should have told her that you love her,' persisted Penelope.

'But she should know how I feel about her by now. It makes no difference to her.'

'Rubbish!' flared Penelope.

He looked pained and bewildered by this abrupt comment.

'What do you mean?' he asked.

'It's rubbish you saying that she should

283

know how you feel without you telling her. How can she know?'

'I've shown her in every way I can think of.'

'In what ways?'

'I've been sympathetic. I've sat with her when she's been too unhappy to speak to me. I've told you before I'm no knight in shining armour, and that I can't go out and slay dragons for her.'

'Could you take her in your arms and kiss her?' demanded Penelope.

'Not unless I thought she wanted me to. I love her too much to make that sort of demand.'

By now they were back at his house and they lingered outside in the damp November twilight. The winds rustled a few dry leaves about their feet and out in the bay the water rippled with silvery light. Someone was coming up the lane, their footsteps crunching on the loose stones.

Penelope, who was trying hard to control an urge to shake Ian because he was so obstinately obtuse, guessed it might be Kathleen coming to do some work in the workshop. Impulsively she took a chance.

'Ian,' she whispered.

He looked down at her. At that moment

she reached up and putting her arms around his neck planted a smacking kiss on his cheek.

It was as if she had given a much-needed cue to an actor. His reaction caught her unawares. His arms swept round her and he kissed her very thoroughly. Held helpless against him, she heard the footsteps stop and then start again as whoever had been approaching turned and went back down the lane.

'Well, Penelope?' said Ian softly. 'Did you get more than you bargained for? You must forgive me. It isn't every day that someone as young and as kind-hearted as yourself offers to kiss me, so when it happens I'm likely to explode.'

'You're forgiven, Ian,' she said with a little laugh. 'But why don't you try kissing Kathleen like that? You might find you get results. There's such a thing as being too gentle, you know.'

She left him, and going down the lane the feeling that she had been there before was very strong. It persisted all the way back to Torvaig. In another life she had had a secret assignation on the hill behind Achmore with a bearded man who had worn a priestly habit. She had been seen by someone who had turned and had gone back down the lane to tell of what she had seen.

Had Kathleen seen Ian kiss her? If so what was her reaction to the sight of another woman in Ian's arms? Penelope grinned to herself. She hoped it had shaken the lovely proud Highlander.

Later the same night she crept downstairs and along the passage to the room which Tearlach called his study, where she hoped to find him alone. The time had come for her to beard the lion in his den again and ask him for the croft at Achmore. In her hand she carried the book he had left in her room the night he had waited for her to return from Inverness.

As she walked through the hallway she was reminded of her first night at Torvaig when she had gone to ask her employer to come and say good night to his nephew. So much had happened since then. She had twisted the lion's tail many times, and he had punished her only once, rather violently and contemptuously, kissing her in a way she would never forget. Otherwise he had been tolerant of her youthful impulsive attacks, and there had been times when he had been very kind.

'Looking for me?' His voice startled her out of her musings.

He was leaning in the doorway of the lounge, a glass of whisky in his hand. He took a sip of it while he waited for her reply.

'Yes.'

'What's the matter? Won't Davy go to sleep?' he jeered.

'I came to return this book to you. You left it in my room. Also I'd like to ask your advice about something, please.'

He looked faintly surprised by her request.

'I'm honoured,' he said with a touch of irony. 'Come in here. We may as well be comfortable.'

He turned back into the lounge and she followed him. She half-expected to find Rosa, dressed in one of her exotic evening dresses, lounging on the big chesterfield, but only the strong fragrance of the Spaniard's scent lingered in the air, bearing witness to the fact that she had left the room recently.

Tearlach told her to sit down, in a gruff voice, and she sat in an armchair, while he flung himself down on the chesterfield. He looked dour and moody and she wondered whether he and Rosa had had a disagreement.

'What do you want advice about?' he asked indifferently.

She laid the book down on the arm of the chair, took a deep breath, looked at him directly and said:

'I want to know if I can have the last remaining croft at Achmore. As the only living descendant of Hector Sandison I believe I can claim it.'

He gave her a long level look, leaned back and took a sip of his whisky before replying.

'You can, provided you can prove that you're a descendant,' he murmured cautiously.

'I have my grandmother's birth certificate which shows she was born here. Is that proof enough?'

His eyes narrowed.

'You've been thinking about this for some time,' he accused.

'Ever since I knew you wouldn't be requiring my services as a nanny any longer.'

'Why?'

'Because I want to stay on Torvaig.'

'And if I refuse to let you have the croft,

what will you do? Find some other way of staying?' he rapped.

She hadn't anticipated that question and had no answer ready, so to avoid his searching glance she looked down at her hands.

'Come, Miss Jones, surely you have an alternative plan? You should never put all your eggs in one basket. It doesn't pay,' he said softly.

He cut to the quick as usual. He was watching her with that narrow-eyed measuring gaze to which he subjected everybody and everything. He would always have an alternative plan as well as an alternative woman, she thought wildly, because it wouldn't pay for him to gamble on one only. Well, she was different.

'No, I haven't an alternative plan. If I can't have the croft, I won't stay,' she said defiantly.

'Will you go to Spain?'

'No.'

'Then where will you go?'

'That's none of your business. Once I leave your employment you're rid of me. That's what you want, isn't it?' she retorted.

This time he didn't have an answer, or if

he did, he didn't say anything. He finished his whisky in one swallow and set the glass down on the long low table in front of the fireplace. Then he gave her another level look.

'All right, you can have a croft,' he said suddenly, and she nearly fell off her chair with surprise. 'How will you pay the rent?'

'I have a little money which my grandmother left me when she died. I think she would like me to use it in this way. I can live on it for a while if I'm careful. I can take in tourists in the summertime and in the winter I think I can find work,' she replied.

'What sort of work?'

'Well, Ian has asked me to do some cleaning for him, and Hugh. . . .'

He held up his hand and interrupted her:

'Wait, wait. You're going a little too fast for me. You mention Ian and Hugh. I suppose they know of your intention to claim a croft?'

'Yes. Really it was Hugh's idea that I should claim one, and when I told Ian, he said he could do with someone to clean and do a little cooking for him,' she replied frankly.

'Then why doesn't he marry you?' he

queried sharply.

'Surely even you know there's more to marriage than a woman just cleaning and cooking for a man,' she retaliated, with counterfeit sweetness.

'Is there?' he questioned ironically. 'Oh, yes, I'd forgotten. You'd require to be loved too, wouldn't you? Doesn't Ian offer enough of that commodity which you consider so precious?'

'I've told you before, he's in love with Kathleen, not with me.'

'I wouldn't have thought so from the way he was behaving this afternoon,' he said slowly, watching her closely.

At first the implication was lost on Penelope and she blinked in puzzlement. Then she noticed the mocking gleam in his eyes and understanding hit her.

'They were your footsteps I heard!' she exclaimed.

'They were. I was coming to call on Ian. Who did you think was coming up the lane?'

'Kathleen.'

'I see. Then that little performance was for her benefit, was it, to show her she has competition?'

'Yes—I mean no.' Penelope's face

burned.

'What exactly do you mean?' he drawled, and she had the impression he was enjoying her discomfiture.

'I mean I'm not competing with Kathleen for Ian,' she almost shouted at him, irritated by the sardonic curve to his mouth. 'Kissing a person doesn't necessarily mean that you're in love with him or her,' she added wildly, and immediately the moments in the car when he had kissed her and she had responded were between them, adding to her confusion and making her cheeks glow a hotter, brighter pink as she saw that sardonic curve to his mouth become a sneer.

'I know that about myself, but I didn't realise it was true of you,' he said curtly. He leaned forward with his elbows on his knees and rested his head in his hands so that she couldn't see the expression on his face any more. 'Let's get back to this business of you having a croft. I suppose you'd like me to tell the Señora that you're not taking the position she offered you?'

'Yes, please.'

'Now the cottage needs renovating before you can live in it. Where do you

292

intend to live while that's being done?' he asked, turning to look at her. The dour expression was back, making him look older and tired, and making her very aware of the differences between them; differences which they had bridged in so many ways on Hallowe'en.

'I don't know. I hadn't thought about it,' she stammered.

'Well, you'd better start thinking fast, because you can't stay here after the end of this week,' he said harshly. 'I shall be accompanying the Usteds to Edinburgh and then to Spain. This house will be closed while I'm away. Mrs. Guthrie is longing to return to her cottage.'

Desolation, grey and arid, was sweeping over her, and she had the utmost difficulty in keeping her head up and hiding her dismay at the thought of him going to Spain. He could only be going for one reason, to be close to Rosa.

'I think Molly Lang will let me stay with her,' she managed to say huskily.

'Good. That's fine. I'll ask someone to start work on the cottage before I leave Torvaig,' he replied coolly. He smiled briefly, impersonally, and stood up. Penelope knew that the interview was at an end.

'Thank you. Good night,' she muttered, and left the room.

Through the hall and up the narrow stairway she went, keeping her mind a blank until she reached her room. There she began to prepare dully for bed and remembered the first night when she had dared to twist the lion's tail. Well, the lion was leaving Torvaig and she was staying. One day he might return and bring with him his wife. One day she might be able to use her training as a nanny for his children, who might have dark hair and dark eyes like the little boy who was sleeping peacefully in the next room.

She climbed into bed and lay awake most of the night, her eyes dry, staring into the darkness, and her heart heavy, aching with an indefinable sadness.

CHAPTER SEVEN

On a dank November day, when the sea was flat and grey and the distant islands seemed like mirages floating above the rim of the horizon, Penelope left the house up on the hill at Achmore, which was still being renovated, and walked slowly down the hill towards the house where Ian McTaggart lived.

A week had passed since Davy and Isa had left Torvaig bound for Spain in the company of Señora Usted, her daughter Rosa and Tearlach. During that week Penelope lived with the Langs and every day had walked up to see her own house, to watch the progress of the workmen, three crofters who were also skilled in roofing, plastering and painting.

Although she was pleased with the work which was being done and was enjoying staying with Molly and making the acquaintance of the other crofters who lived in Cladach and Achmore, she was conscious of a flatness of spirit; a flatness which had descended upon her the night she had asked Tearlach for the croft; a flatness which was like the sea that day, stretching grey and empty away to nothing.

She had seen Tearlach several times since that night, before he had left with the Usteds and the children, but she knew she had really said good-bye to him that night when she had said good night. On the day of their departure she had felt no wrench at parting from Davy and Isa, but the sight of Tearlach's shaggy head disappearing into the interior of the black car as he had taken his seat behind the steering wheel had made her throat go suddenly dry. Unbidden tears had sprung to her eyes and she had hurried away from the window from which she had been watching.

He had gone from the island and once more the big house was empty and desolate, and she had the most peculiar feeling that he would never return. The lion had left Torvaig for ever.

Penelope sighed and squared her shoulders. Well, she was on Torvaig to stay. She had a house and land. She was free, healthy and strong. No man was her master and she was slave to no one, not even to those strange flashbacks, which had now stopped. How many other young women of her age could say that they were independent in the way she was, as they toiled away in the cities at typewriters, in hairdressing salons or in classrooms?

She decided that she would call on Hugh and ask him if he had any ideas about where she could acquire some furniture for her house, and after that she would go and help Molly with some sewing.

She was just approaching Ian's house when Kathleen came up the lane from the other direction. They met almost at the door to the workshop. Beneath the hood of the cloak of bright green wool which Kathleen was wearing with that grace and elegance which were hers alone, the fine-boned face was sharp and pale, and Penelope was shocked to see how much weight Kathleen had lost since the last time she had seen her.

'I'm told you are going to live on the hills,' said Kathleen politely.

'Yes, I should be able to move in soon,' replied Penelope.

'Why do you want to stay on Torvaig, of all places?' asked Kathleen curiously.

'Because I feel I belong here,' said Penelope coolly. What other reason could there be? she found herself thinking.

'Feel you belong?' queried Kathleen with a touch of mockery, and she arched her lovely white neck and laughed. 'Oh, yes you've been here before, haven't you? You *felt* you came here in a Viking ship. How well I remember Tearlach's amusement that night when he told us of your vision of the past. He didn't want you here then, and he went to a lot of trouble to get rid of you, short of sacking you outright. But you're not going after all and so he has had to remove himself.'

The colour drained out of Penelope's face. Surely she had not looked as if she had been chasing the laird?

'I find it quite ridiculous that a city sparrow like you should feel she belongs to an island in the Hebrides,' scoffed Kathleen. Pain and disappointment had turned her into a sneering shrew, thought Penelope, and if she went on like this much longer she would lose all that beauty and grace which were her inheritance.

'No more ridiculous than I find the idea of you, a country hen, going to settle in the big city,' she retorted. 'You'll soon be lost.'

'Who told you that I'm going to live in the city?' asked Kathleen sharply.

'Ian did. He says that after the exhibition of your work you won't be returning here. You'll be staying in London.'

Kathleen's face seemed to go paler and tauter than ever as her pride stepped in to help her conceal her true feelings, and suddenly Penelope felt sorry for her.

'He's very worried about you,' she said impulsively, speaking as she felt.

Kathleen's fine eyes flashed with golden

fire.

'Who is?' she demanded.

'Ian. He has been ever since you went to Edinburgh with Mr. Gunn. You see, he loves you very much and he was afraid you might be hurt.'

'Loves me!' exclaimed Kathleen, a faint pink colour touching her cheeks. 'But he's never given any sign of loving me. He just sits there more interested in twisting silver than in me. He's always been the same. There was a time in the spring when I thought. . . .' She broke off and bit her lower lip. 'You must be mistaken,' she added stiffly.

'No, I'm not. Just because he's quiet and patient and can't slay dragons for you, you mustn't think he doesn't love you,' persisted Penelope. 'His is the sort of love which grows slowly, but lasts for ever.'

'Why are you telling me all this? I thought you were attracted to him and that's why you want to stay at Achmore. You've spent many hours with him lately, and the day I returned from London I saw you and him in his workshop. You looked well *together*, and I know you share an interest in the past. I have to admit I was unhappy about the way Tearlach treated me in London. He was so cutting and sarcastic, and oh, so right. You see, I'd been doing what my mother suggested.'

'What was that?'

'She suggested that I should make myself indispensable to Tearlach. He had told her when he returned to Scotland that he would like to settle down, that it was time he had a home. She was annoyed with him for coming back and more or less snatching Torvaig from under her nose and she suggested I seduce him and make him marry me. The idea appealed to me. Tearlach is an attractive man and I knew that as his wife I would be well treated even if he never loved me. Also at the time I felt I would never know a man's love. Ian seemed disinterested, and I supposed having reached my thirtieth birthday I was getting a bit desperate.' Kathleen paused and her eyes narrowed as if she were in pain. 'But Tearlach saw through my attempts to inveigle him and I came running home to Ian for comfort, only to find he had a new friend in you.'

'So that's why you've been unhappy, stalking about like a tragedy queen,' exclaimed Penelope. 'How silly of you!'

Kathleen's mouth twisted into a travesty

300

of a smile.

'I once said that to you. Do you remember?' she murmured. 'Yes, I have been silly. Oh, the time I've wasted in my life waiting for someone to sweep me off my feet with his love, and all the time Ian has been waiting too,' she cried, suddenly dropping her pride. 'I'm not going to waste any more. Excuse me, please, and thank you.'

She opened the door of the workshop and hurried through it, leaving it swinging. Penelope could hear her calling to Ian, and with a smile she closed the door and went on her way down the lane to Hugh's house.

She found him sorting through his canvases, choosing which ones he would take to Edinburgh. Quickly she told him what had just happened.

'A fairy godmother, that's who you are. Now I shan't mind leaving Kath here. How is the house?' he said.

'I should be able to move in next week, if I have any furniture by then.'

'I'll take you over to Invercol tomorrow. You should be able to pick up some pieces at the weekly auction there. If you find anything we can bring it back in the van,' said Hugh, and Penelope thought what a

301

good friend he had been to her ever since she had come to Torvaig. In fact if it hadn't been for Hugh she might never have come and might not have been able to stay.

'Do you think I'll be able to manage the croft?' she asked him hesitantly, betraying the uncertainty which was in her mind.

'With some help from your neighbours, I think you will,' he answered serenely. 'That's what is so wonderful about living on Torvaig. We all help one another. It's a real community. Before Tearlach came back I was thinking of going to live in one of those communes with some friends of mine in an old house, but Torvaig has been a much better experience. Do you know what Tearlach said to me the last time I saw him?'

'How could I know? I wasn't there,' she retorted.

'He said he'd decided to let you have your croft because it had occurred to him that there are far too many single men on the island to make it a really balanced community, and that single women would have to be encouraged to live here. He thought he would make a start by allowing you to have your croft. He said he wouldn't be surprised if you weren't married before you'd been at Achmore twelve months, and that in eighteen months you'd be acting as nanny to your own baby,' said Hugh with a chuckle. 'Hey, Penny, what are you doing with that paint? Be careful! Tearlach said it, not me. You do get upset easily, don't you?'

Having chased him round the room with the paintbrush in the way he had once chased her, Penelope collapsed in a chair and for the next half hour sat watching Hugh paint while she thought up devastating retorts to be delivered to Tearlach Gunn the next time she saw him. Only there might never be a next time, she realised forlornly.

As she had hoped, she was able to move into her cottage within three days. There was still much work to be done, but at least the kitchen and the living room were habitable. Hugh was there with the few pieces of furniture they had managed to pick up at Invercol, and he helped her to carry it in and put it in position. He was, as usual, very talkative, full of the good news that Ian and Kathleen had gone to Inverness to be married.

'In a register office, much to Mother's disgust. She wanted Kath in white with all the trimmings, which is only natural since Kath is her only daughter. But can you imagine Kath in white doing all the right things, or Ian in a morning suit? I hope when I get married Mother will have realised that such conventions are unpopular with me and that she won't even try to persuade the girl I'm going to marry to have a white wedding,' he said.

'But I thought marriage was out as far as you're concerned,' said Penelope, with an air of sweet innocence. 'I thought you were going to be a bachelor all your life with a few special women friends on the side.'

He grinned at her and cocked his head to one side.

'Sometimes, when I come across someone like you, I think how pleasant it would be if you didn't have to go back to Torvaig House, or the Langs, or wherever you happen to be staying for the night, when I've plenty of room in my cottage for a lodger,' he teased. 'And I start thinking how nice it would be if meals were always cooked well and served on time just when a man is needing some food instead of him having to stop work and start scavenging for it.'

'You're as bad as your beastly cousin! He

thinks that's all wives are for, cleaning and cooking,' retorted Penelope, remembering Tearlach asking her why Ian didn't marry her if he wanted her to cook and clean for him.

'I'm thinking he's wishing he had a wife at this very moment,' Hugh said casually, giving her a shrewd sidelong glance. She was putting up the curtains she had made for the kitchen on Molly Lang's sewing machine, but at his words she turned, her face expressing the strange feeling of apprehension which had her in its grip.

'Didn't I tell you that Tearlach's back?' added Hugh even more casually.

'At Torvaig House?' she whispered.

'Yes. He came yesterday, from the hospital in Edinburgh.'

'Hospital? Oh, Hugh, stop being so tantalising! What was he doing in hospital?' she demanded, dropping a curtain in the sink thoughtlessly, too worried by what he had said to notice.

'There was an accident,' he said curtly, and watched the colour fade from her cheeks, leaving them paper white. 'Young Davy ran away down some steps at the Castle. Tearlach went after him, slipped and fell. He cracked a couple of ribs. The

305

Usteds and the children went on to Spain without him. After three days in hospital he came back here to hole up in his den and lick his wounds, like old lions do. I met Mrs. Guthrie in the village and she told me. She's been in to see him, but says he isn't in a very good mood, and she's worried because she can't stay to look after him because.... Hey, where do you think you're going?'

Penelope was pulling on her anorak over her blue highnecked sweater, zipping it up and then pushing her hands into blue woollen mitts and cramming a blue knitted beret on her dark shining hair. Her knitted blue and white checked skirt swirled around her shapely thighs, clad in long blue stockings, as she made for the door.

'I'm going to Torvaig House, of course. Where do you think?' she snapped at Hugh, wondering why he should be so obtuse. 'Your cousin is hurt and there's no one to help him, so I must.'

'Wait a minute!' Hugh's big hands were on her shoulders stopping her, and his bright tawny eyes searched her pale, big-eyed wedge of a face. 'There's half a gale blowing and it'll take you hours to walk there.'

Penelope tilted her chin and her blue eyes sparkled with determination.

'I'm still going,' she said, trying to free herself from his hands.

Seeing that determination Hugh accepted his defeat with a sigh and a faintly rueful grin as he realised that he had never had a chance with this small, impulsive whirlwind of a girl. He released her and, picking up his sheepskin jacket from the chair where he had thrown it, shrugged into it.

'I'll drive you over,' he said crisply. 'I must say I felt a bit sorry for the old lion myself when I heard he'd been hurt. It's put paid to his courting of Rosa Usted for a while. I wonder if he'll ever marry.'

'I wish you wouldn't call him old,' said Penelope impatiently. 'Hurry up, if you want to take me.'

He drove along the road as fast as he dared in his old van. Beside him Penelope sat tense, staring out at the tossing windswept water, her mind and her heart already ahead of her in Torvaig House with Tearlach Gunn.

'Have you done this before, in that other lifetime of yours?' asked Hugh, suddenly flicking a curious glance in her direction.

'No, this is all new,' she said slowly, as if she had come back to the van from somewhere far away. 'I haven't had a flashback since Mr. Gunn left Torvaig to go to Spain. How strange! In the last one, I felt as if he'd gone away and would never be coming back.'

'Who is *he?*'

'Why, my.... I mean the slave girl's husband, I suppose,' stammered Penelope, her face flushing as she felt confused.

'That fits in with the legend,' said Hugh. 'He went away on one of his trading expeditions and didn't return. Lost at sea, presumably, or in a fight.'

'Yes, it does fit in, doesn't it?' she murmured faintly. 'Hugh, how badly hurt is Mr. Gunn?'

'Not badly, or he'd still be in hospital. Have you fallen for the old ... I mean Tearlach?'

'Am I in love with him? I don't know. I'm all confused. He can be as exasperating and as tantalising as you,' she replied evenly, not really wishing to tell him how she felt.

'Then why are you rushing off to help him?'

'Because he helped me when I fainted,

and when I had the 'flu germ he was awfully kind. The least I can do is help him when he's down.'

'That sounds reasonable enough,' murmured Hugh, noting that she had gone pale and tense again, and drawing his own conclusions.

They drove up to the front door of Torvaig House with a rattle, and the van had hardly stopped when Penelope was out of it and running round to the side door, clutching her hat on with one hand in case the tearing wind pulled it from her head. Down the passage she ran to the kitchen and bounced off Mrs. Guthrie's ample bosom as the housekeeper was leaving the room.

'Ach, it's yourself, then,' exclaimed Mrs. Guthrie. 'What are you wanting here?'

'I've come to look after Mr. Gunn,' said Penelope breathlessly, taking off her anorak and throwing it on a kitchen chair. Hats and mitts followed it as she pretended she hadn't noticed the strange look Mrs. Guthrie gave Hugh as he came into the room. 'Where is he?' she demanded.

'In bed, where he should be, resting,' said Mrs. Guthrie, with a snap. 'And the job I had persuading him to go there, and him three sheets to the wind, I'm thinking, with all the whisky he's been drinking. To ease the pain in his chest, he said,' she grumbled with a scornful growl. 'Ach, wait now, Penelope. You can't go up there. It isn't proper for a young woman like you to be visiting a man in his bedroom.'

At this point Hugh intervened to offer to take Mrs. Guthrie to the ferry because he knew she wanted to go to the mainland to see her daughter, and not waiting to hear any more cautionary remarks, Penelope sped out of the room to the hall. Up the front stairs she bounded. At the top of them she paused for breath, listening to the pounding of her heart. Then she walked quietly to the door of Tearlach's room. It was open and she could see a lamp was on, making a warm pool of amber light in the purple gloom of the wild November afternoon.

She stepped into the room and closed the door quietly behind her, then went over to the bed. Tearlach was lying flat on his back. He hadn't bothered to undress and was lying on top of the crimson bedcover. Under the tumble of blond-streaked hair his face was pale and seemed thinner. A frown of pain made a dark line between his eyebrows. His eyes were closed, but she could tell by the firm set of his mouth that he was not asleep.

The sight of him made her heart feel as if it would burst. She longed to fling her arms around him and hold him close, and in that moment she recognised that it was love for him that had sent her hurrying through the bleak wintry day to be by his side.

'Mr. Gunn,' she said softly.

He opened one eye, looked at her, closed it again and groaned, turning his head restlessly on the pillow.

'Oh, what is it?' gasped Penelope. 'Are you in pain?'

'Yes,' he murmured.

'What can I do to help you?'

'Sit down and hold my hand.' This time his voice seemed stronger and there was the suspicion of a laugh in it. Eyeing him warily she sat down on the edge of the bed. Immediately one of his hands grasped one of hers. There was nothing wrong with the strength of his grasp, she thought, wincing a little as long muscular fingers closed round hers.

'Where is the pain?' she asked.

'Everywhere,' he replied. 'Why have you come?'

'I came to help you because Hugh said Mrs. Guthrie was worried about you and she can't stay to help you.'

'But why should you come and look after me?' he asked. His eyes were open now, dark and unfathomable in the subdued lighting.

'Once you looked after me, when I fainted, and then when I had stomach 'flu you were very kind, so I thought this would be a good chance to repay my debt to you.'

He closed his eyes, groaned again and his fingers lost their grip on hers. Not knowing what to make of his behaviour, half suspicious, thinking that he might be playing on her sympathy for his own amusement, she said agitatedly:

'I thought you said the pain would go away if you held my hand.'

'I did, but it's come back.'

'Did they give you any pills to kill the pain when you left hospital?'

'I suppose they did. I can't remember. I prefer whisky,' he murmured.

'So Mrs. Guthrie told me,' she commented dryly. 'But obviously it isn't having any effect. Where might the pills be? Shall I look for them?'

She tried to withdraw her hand from his,

but his fingers tightened again. Their strength was astonishing in someone who was supposed to be in pain, rousing her suspicions even more. She remembered Hugh once saying that Tearlach was not above putting on an act when he wanted to deceive someone.

'No, stay where you are,' he ordered curtly. 'The pain is going away again. It came back only because I didn't like your answer to my question. You don't have to pay any debt to me. I didn't look after you when you fainted and had the 'flu because I expected repayment. I'm glad you've come, though. I haven't been very good company for myself, I hate being ill.'

'Everyone does,' she comforted him. 'How did it happen?'

'We went to Edinburgh from here. The Usteds wanted to stop in Princes Street and to see the Castle and Holyrood Palace. The day we went to the Castle Davy behaved abominably. I think he was beginning to realise that he wasn't going to see you again.'

He closed his eyes again and the frown line came back.

'He hadn't known me for very long, so why should he be upset?' she asked.

313

'You know how he used to behave when he couldn't have me dancing attendance on him? Well, he was acting in the same way, only it was you he wanted. Anyway, there we were, Rosa and I, with him in tow, looking at the place. It was the wrong time of the year, damned cold, with the wind off the Pentland Hills doing its usual good job of penetrating even the thickest tweed,' he remarked with a wry twist to his mouth. 'Rosa kept wishing she was in Spain, and I kept wishing . . .'

He broke off. The frown deepened, but she was sure that it wasn't produced by physical pain this time. She wondered if he was regretting having taken Rosa to see the Castle in Edinburgh because the visit had led indirectly to him being separated from the lovely Spaniard.

'Davy ran away down some steps,' he continued tersely. 'I went after him, fell, cracked my ribs and knocked myself out. It was a damned foolish thing to do.'

Self-disgust thickened his voice and he turned his head restlessly on the pillow again. This time, when his fingers tightened on her hand, Penelope returned the pressure as her foolish heart went out to him.

'But why did the Usteds go to Spain without you?' she asked.

'I asked them to. Rosa wanted to stay, but Davy was restless and I decided that in the long run it would be better if the break with me was made then and there, a clean cutting off of the relationship. So she and the Señora flew to London the next day with the children, and on to Spain.'

'You must have been very disappointed.'

He opened his eyes to scowl with puzzlement at her.

'Why should I?'

'Because you couldn't go to Spain.'

'I was only going because, in the first place, I had thought it might be easier for the children if I went.' Then he saw disbelief expressed on her face and his eyes began to twinkle. 'Oho,' he said softly, 'you had me paired off with the dark and beautiful Rosa, did you? It looks as if my little act was too convincing.'

Her glance was wide and bewildered.

'Was it an act?' she asked sweetly, and he grinned at her and squeezed her hand too hard as a form of punishment, so that she cried out.

'Yes, it was, although I have to admit as in the case of Kathleen, I was temporarily attracted. Rosa is an intelligent woman, but too amenable for my taste, and she has an aggravating way of agreeing with everything I say. I prefer to have a few hot arguments with my women. Argument lends spice to the lovemaking. Don't you agree, Penelope?'

The colour rose in her cheeks and she avoided meeting his eyes.

'If I agree with you you'll be suspicious of me and think I'm being amenable. If I don't agree, I won't be telling the truth,' she retorted, and he began to laugh, only to stop as he remembered his cracked ribs.

'Oh, hell,' he muttered. 'Why did I ever go after that little devil?'

'How did you get back to Torvaig?' she asked, looking at him anxiously. This time she knew he wasn't shamming pain because it was there in his face, carving new lines down his cheeks and round his mouth.

'I discharged myself and drove here.'

'Oh, Tearlach!' The name slipped out without her realising and his eyes half-opened. He smiled at her as he corrected her pronunciation of the Gaelic version of his name. 'You might have damaged yourself permanently,' she continued anxiously. 'I'd better go and ring up Dr.

316

Farquhar and ask him to come and examine you.'

'No, not yet. I'll be all right. Besides, there's a lot to talk about.'

'But it's hurting you to talk.'

'Then you talk and I'll listen, for once. Tell me about Kathleen and Ian. Mrs. Guthrie has been muttering something about them getting married and about how foolish I am to let such a lovely young woman escape.'

She told him what had happened and when she had finished he gave her a shrewd probing glance.

'Are you unhappy about Ian?' he asked abruptly.

'Of course not. Kathleen was surprised when I told her that he loves her. She had always hoped he did, but when he showed no signs of telling her, it turned her off and she became desperate. That's why she fell in with her mother's plan that she should try and marry you. As Hugh put it, rather crudely, she was ripe for the picking.'

'Don't I know it,' he muttered. 'And I didn't want to be the one to pick her. If I had it would have been all over between us within six months.'

For a while there was silence in the

317

room. Outside the wind whistled and rattled at the window. Penelope glanced at Tearlach. He seemed to be asleep, so she tried to withdraw her hand from his again. She almost had it free when his fingers curled relentlessly round hers.

'Where are you going?' he asked.

'To see if Hugh has come back.'

'Do you want him to come back and stay here with you?' he asked.

'Perhaps it would be better if he did, in case you need help.'

'But I thought you'd come to help me?'

'I have, but I couldn't lift you or help you to dress,' she said, a little confused by the glint in his eyes.

'I can dress myself, thank you, and I'm not in such a bad way that I can't move,' he replied with a touch of impatience. 'I meant do you want Hugh to stay here because you like having him near you?'

'No, I don't want him.'

'That's a relief. If he were here, he'd only cramp my style as he did on the yacht coming up from Mallaig,' muttered Tearlach obscurely. 'I can do without his youthful competition. How do you like your cottage at Achmore?'

'Very much.'

'Would you be willing to share it?'

'It would depend on the person,' she said slowly. 'It's going to be my home, and although I'd be willing to take in tourists during the summer, I'm not sure whether I'd want to have just anyone living with me permanently.'

'I can appreciate your feelings,' he said. 'For many years I didn't have a home of my own, but I always wanted one. Then I learned that I'd inherited this island. I came here, saw this house and decided to make it my home. I spent a great deal of money on things to make it comfortable. I'd lived here on and off almost two years before I realised that it was no more home to me than any other place I'd lived in over the years. So I sold it.'

His announcement came as a shock. For a few seconds she could only stare at him in bewilderment. Then the questions came tumbling out.

'When? Why? Who has bought it?'

'Andrew Pollock, who was one of my guests here at the end of August. He's a scion of a well-known Scottish family which owns a brewery. He's made a career of the hotel business and has a chain of hotels, all in attractive areas of Scotland where there hasn't been adequate hotel accommodation before.'

'Hugh said you'd always thought Torvaig needed a hotel,' she said.

'I could have turned the house into one myself, but Andrew will make a better job of it because he knows what he's doing. Every man to his trade,' he murmured.

'What is your trade?' she asked.

'Taking chances,' he replied enigmatically, then seeing that she wasn't satisfied with his answer he added, 'Speculating. Buying something the value of which, I think, will increase and then selling it at a profit.' He paused, seeing a troubled frown on her face.

'Even your home?' she asked.

'I know you don't approve,' he replied harshly, 'but I am what I am and it's the only talent I have. I try to use it to the best of my ability, and sometimes, I hope, to the benefit of others. A hotel on the island will benefit its tourist trade considerably.'

'But where are you going to live?'

'I'm not sure. I've never been sure. That's why I had to do something about Davy and Isa. Always at the back of my mind was my knowledge of myself. I was already getting tired of Torvaig when Avis was killed. I didn't want them to become too attached to me because I knew I would have to find them a more stable home with their other relatives. Do you understand?'

'Yes, I understand now,' she said quietly, thinking back to the number of times she had accused him of not loving the children. She was beginning to realise that he knew more about the meaning of the word love than she did. He dealt in realities, not romances, but that did not mean he was not motivated by love.

'Do you remember Hallowe'en?' he asked suddenly, and there was a hint of desperation in his manner now. She nodded, feeling the warmth creep into her cheeks.

'I do too,' he said. 'I walked into the kitchen and found you sitting there. You invited me to the dance, and suddenly that something which had always been lacking in this house, in fact in my whole life, seemed to be there.'

'Oh, what was it?' she demanded, her interest caught.

'I thought, I hoped it was love. Your sort of love for me. The sort of love which you give to a person no matter how old or how wealthy or how rude he is, which doesn't care where he comes from or where he's going. On Hallowe'en it changed a cheerless dump for furniture into a home for the first time, too late because I'd sold it.'

'Oh, not too late,' she assured him quickly. 'Home is where the heart is. It has nothing to do with bricks and mortar. My grandmother always said that.'

'And where is your heart?' He seemed to pounce on her words.

'Wherever you are, as if you didn't know,' she said with a touch of asperity which brought the teasing grin back to his face. 'That is why I'm here this afternoon. But I've only just found out, so please don't rush me,' she added breathlessly, as she realised how much she had committed herself.

He sank back against the pillows and let out a deep sigh of satisfaction.

'I thought I'd never get you to admit it! Don't worry, I shan't be rushing anyone until these ribs are healed. Anyway, wooing you is something I intend to take my time over. I want to enjoy it. I've given up "gathering rosebuds", to quote that poem Kathleen told us about. This is for ever as far as I'm concerned, but if you don't feel

322

like that, let's call quits before we take any vows to love and to cherish.'

'I'd like it to be for keeps too,' she said shyly.

'That's the answer I wanted,' he replied, 'but don't go all amenable, will you, Penelope? I love you because you're you and you dare to twist the lion's tail. Hallowe'en was a moment of truth for me, but I couldn't be sure of you. I thought your heart was with Ian. When you returned my kisses I thought you were using me as a substitute for him. That made me angry and I was rough with you. Then you wanted Achmore, to be near him, I thought. I saw you kiss him, and in spite of what you said later, I was convinced you were in love with him. There was nothing to keep me here any longer, so I decided to go to Spain.'

'You weren't coming back. You'd gone for good,' she accused, remembering how clearly she had felt he would never return.

'Yes, and I might not be here if it wasn't for Davy. I suppose I ought to be grateful to the brat, just as I should be grateful to Hugh for interfering that day at Mallaig when I wanted to send you back to London. Do you realise we might never have known each other?'

'I refuse to believe that. I had come to Torvaig. I'd have come some other way,' she replied earnestly.

'We'll argue about that another time,' he said, with an amused glint in his eyes, 'At the moment there are much more attractive things I want to do.'

'Why did you come back?' she persisted, refusing to be put off by the altered touch of his fingers which were not holding her hand tightly, but caressing the inside of her wrist, sending queer little tingles up her arm.

'In hospital I had time to think. I don't give up easily, but there I could see I was doing just that, giving up before I'd really tried. I'd found you, the only woman I've ever known with whom I wanted to stay, and I'd run away rather than be hurt by watching you love another man. I was giving up without a fight. I was furious with myself. I had to come back to try to win you away from Ian because I knew that if I didn't I'd be homeless for the rest of my life. My instinct to return here was right, and when I saw you walk in here this afternoon I realised I might not have to fight very hard. Penelope, do you think you could bear to share your cottage with me? After the end of November I'll have nowhere to live.'

'I'm sure I can,' she replied joyfully, her eyes shining with love. Then she added, in all innocence, as her practicality asserted itself, 'What a good thing I've bought a double bed!'

Tearlach wanted to laugh, but he couldn't, so he groaned instead and closed his eyes. Immediately she leaned forward anxiously to push the hair back from his brow and to smooth away the line of pain. When he didn't respond she tried to withdraw, only to find that his other arm had crept round her and that she was being held down, close to him. His eyes opened and invitation gleamed in them. Desire flamed within her in answer to that invitation. Giving in to it, she touched his mouth with her own and was lost.

This time no curious moon peered in at the window. As the minutes lengthened no one opened the door to disturb them, and in the words of Penelope's favourite story about the return of the Last of the Heroes to his wife: 'He held her in his arms, and in the happiness of that moment it seemed that all his wanderings were but little things compared with so true and great a joy.'

Photoset, printed and bound in Great Britain by REDWOOD BURN LIMITED, Trowbridge, Wiltshire